THREE
DAYS

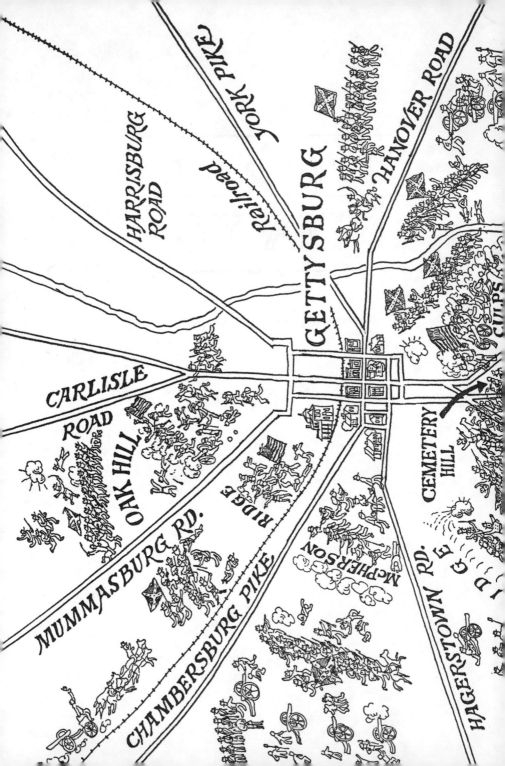

BATTLE of GETTYSBURG
JULY 1-3, 1863

ROSENBLUM.

BALTIMORE PIKE

N

TANEYTOWN RD.

CEMETERY RIDGE

LITTLE ROUND TOP

BIG ROUND TOP

WHEATFIELD

PEACH ORCHARD

DEVILS DEN

EMMITSBURG RD.

SEMINARY

THREE DAYS

by **Paxton Davis**

Atheneum 1980 *New York*

LIBRARY OF CONGRESS CATALOGING IN PUBLICATION DATA

Davis, Paxton, date
Three days.

SUMMARY: Describes the battle of Gettysburg
through the eyes of Robert E. Lee,
following that great general from his entry
into Pennsylvania to the disastrous conclusion
for the Confederate troops.
1. Gettysburg, Battle of, 1863—Juvenile fiction.
[1. Gettysburg, Battle of, 1863—Fiction.
2. United States—History—Civil War,
1861-1865—Campaigns and battles—Fiction.
3. Lee, Robert Edward, 1807-1870—Fiction]
I. Title.
PZ7.D2975Th   [Fic]   79-22676
ISBN 0-689-30764-0

Published simultaneously in Canada by
McClelland & Stewart, Ltd.
Manufactured by R. R. Donnelley & Sons,
Crawfordsville, Indiana
Maps by Richard Rosenblum
Designed by M. M. Ahern
First Edition

For
Peggy
with
Love

Contents

That moment would linger and shine
in the American memory forever, the
terrible unforgettable moment of truth
that would symbolize inexpressible
things. It blotted out other scenes then,
and it still does.

Bruce Catton: *This Hallowed Ground*

Prologue

{ *June 30, 1863* }

THE LAND WAS LUSH HERE, tilled and tamed by generations of hardy Pennsylvania farmers to yield a ripe abundance of wheat and corn, apples and peaches and milk and beef; and to the thousands of Confederate soldiers streaming eastward down its market roads and country lanes it seemed another Eden after the waste and desolation to which two years of increasingly bitter warfare had reduced Virginia. The fields were green, the cattle plump, and the stone and frame barns so sturdy, with their trim lines, spacious lofts and crisp fresh paint, they might have passed for houses in the scrub country of Georgia and Alabama and Mississippi and Texas; and overhead, undarkened yet by the ceaseless smoke of battle from which they'd come, the sky was blue and clear in the hot summer midday, with here and there a bright white cloud like a cotton boll. From the farmyards and fence rails the people watched them glumly, silently, but raised no hindrance to their progress; while for themselves, as much by inclination as instruction, they kept their pace and order, stepping briskly along in their endless columns with few words for those beyond their immediate ranks. Resentment at these invaders' presence the Pennsylvanians might feel, but they kept it to themselves; elation at apparent triumph over a powerful enemy was the Confederates' part, but they refrained from giving it vent. On east they tramped, bound for glory, red dust rising about them and hanging there, to catch the sunlight, miles backward toward Chambersburg.

Yet for all their discipline they made a motley picture. They walked like pack mules, but most were barefoot. They carried their bedrolls, canteens and cartridge belts neatly, their muskets as if on parade, but they themselves were filthy. Their lines were perfect, their cadence crisp, but few wore real uniforms at all, attired instead in such scraps and rags of coarse woolen homespun as they could beg or pilfer, shirts and jeans dyed ten thousand hues of butternut by ten thousand different hands. Something pulled them together, though, some intangible power that passed from man to man despite their hungry faces and scarecrow clothes, and it gave them such vitality the Pennsylvanians drew back as they passed, as if from a great wave or the onrush of a mighty wind. They were worn men, men thinned and hardened and with arms burned black by the elements, but few who saw them could believe them less than invincible. Lee's men, Lee's legions: the Army of Northern Virginia was on the march, and none to halt it.

Or so it seemed. That his soldiers could do anything

4

within reasonable expectation their commander, now riding forward amongst them, could not doubt; yet an unspoken apprehension nagged at him too. This was Lee, Robert E. Lee, gray-bearded, gray clad and mounted as always upon his gray horse Traveller, since the Seven Days' Battles outside Richmond exactly a year before, their commander and increasingly their hero as well—the South's hero, in fact, and the world's, so far the single soldier of the war to capture the imagination and warm the blood of men everywhere—for many, a man who could do no wrong. Yet Lee knew otherwise. Despite the modesty and simplicity of his dress and manner, he was in war the incarnation of the doctrine of initiative and attack whose invariable impulse was to carry the fight to the enemy; and now at last, striking his boldest blow yet, it seemed to him possible that his audacity might have outstripped his capabilities.

His plan held much promise, at any rate. He had drawn the Yankees at Antietam and trounced them at Fredericksburg; and at Chancellorsville, little more than a month past, he had won the enormous tactical victory many considered his masterpiece, effecting in the end the classic double envelopment sought by ambitious generals since Hannibal's at Cannae. Yet concealed within the apparent triumph lay the grim truth that, though his losses were smaller than the Union's, his resources were smaller still; eventually, since the North could replace its dead and wounded and the South could not, simple arithmetic must overtake his armies. The paradox was cruel but clear: if the war went on, he would lose for winning.

He must end it, then: must strike decisively, mortally and where the Union expected it least, at its rear, in its own backyard, thus—by bringing the enemy to bay, if not to its knees—forcing the conflict to a conclusion less destructive to the South than if longer protracted. To attack was his nature anyway, the mode of warfare for which every instinct he possessed was ready, and he had demonstrated its effectiveness repeatedly, never more vividly than when, the September before, he'd sown chaos across the North by invading Maryland and battling ferociously, if inconclusively, at Antietam; but a fresh foray northward held forth hope of additional rewards. Movement would draw the war and the enemy away from Virginia soil at the crucial season when crops must be harvested, as well as restore to his army, anchored too long below the Rappahannock, its famous flexibility; while, though to threaten Washington would be achievement enough, with speed, secrecy and luck he might take it altogether and thus deal the Union a deathblow—for Confederate conquest of the Federal capital must prompt swift British and French recognition of the South as a sovereign nation. A negotiated peace could not help but follow.

So he had argued and so, with but a single dissent, the Confederate Cabinet had agreed, President Davis enthusiastically; and so the thing had been ordered: a second wholesale invasion of the Union, this time by moving

6

his men north through the gaps of the Blue Ridge and down the protected roads of the Shenandoah Valley, thence eastward and southward across Pennsylvania to strike whatever targets opportunity offered . . . a surprised Army of the Potomac, perhaps, caught napping again, perhaps Philadelphia or Baltimore; perhaps Washington itself.

A gamble? No doubt, but the prize justified it; and here beside him, moving on Cashtown in a seemingly endless butternut column, strode his surest protection against loss—an army so stalwart its feats were passing into legend while battles remained for its winning. They had yet to fail him, his soldiers, Virginians, Carolinians, boys from Georgia and Tennessee, the Gulf States and Texas; and now, silently, almost reverently, they raised their hats as he passed.

Meanwhile he'd insured himself. In the wake of Chancellorsville and its terrible losses—one still too painful to contemplate—he'd reorganized his command, and it was through that new disposition of force that he'd planned the campaign and set in motion the long march north to initiate it. Each of his three reconstructed infantry corps was led by a general of demonstrated grit, as was each of its three constituent divisions and each division's brigades; and though his foot soldiers numbered but sixty thousand, unarguably they were the world's toughest and best, all sinew and bone. Dick Ewell went first, the army's crustiest eccentric, "Old Bald Head" to his men, a leg lighter since Groveton but not a whit less

7

opinionated, leading his corps up out of Culpeper by way of Front Royal in the valley, then fighting brilliantly at Winchester and pushing on so rapidly afterward, through Martinsburg and Hagerstown, that by now, as the left tentacle of Lee's proposed envelopment, he and his troops awaited instruction deep in the Union rear at Carlisle and York. James Longstreet had followed, Lee's own "Old Warhorse," massively built and bearded and as imperturbably obdurate as the mules of his native Georgia, crossing the Potomac with his corps at Williamsport and now on the march out of Chambersburg. Last north was A. P. Hill, "Little Powell" of the red whiskers and explosive temper, new to corps command but old to combat and today, with Heth's division out front, the point of Lee's eastward assault on Pennsylvania.

So—climax of a march rivaling Xenophon's—the army had gathered, or was gathering, and would concentrate presently; yet Lee, who'd ordained it, retained an inescapable disquiet. Part came from himself: since a terrible throat catarrh in March he'd suffered repeated spells of pain in the chest, back and arms, aftermath of an inflammation of the heart sac, the doctors warned, and though he'd returned promptly to duty it was a duty he found physically more and more difficult, now and then speechless with pain and afterward vague of thought and feebler of will; nor, after so many years of robust health and self-sufficiency, could he bring himself to complain. His corps commanders worried him too, able men all but unproven at higher authority: could Ewell strike when he should, Hill hold back when he shouldn't? Could the stalwart Longstreet stir from his constitutional slowness and move swiftly if urged to? Conundrums, enigmas, and only battle would tell. Meanwhile a deeper difficulty underlay all: he faced whatever was to come bereft of arm and eye.

The arm was Jackson, the invincible Stonewall, dead a month of his wounds from Chancellorsville and—what Lee could have said of no one else—indispensable and irreplaceable; not a lovable man, too rigid and implacable to laugh or cry or accept the simple pleasures of ordinary friendship, but an officer whose vision, imagination and executive grasp needed only Lee's most general strategic intention to effect tactical triumph; they'd fought like a single organism, Lee proposing, Jackson disposing, and now the organism was halved, if not worse.

His unease went deeper yet, however. If Jackson's death meant the loss of his right arm, as he'd mourned after Chancellorsville, he was blind now as well, eyeless in mid-campaign, and for that the blame fell on Jeb Stuart, wherever he was . . . and with himself, truth be told, for letting the young buck spring free. That Stuart had grown and was growing as commander of the cavalry corps was undeniable, for he'd grasped quickly enough—what all those showy mounted charges so popular with his instructors at West Point had failed dismally to make clear—that the essential function of cavalry is to screen the in-

9

fantry's flanks and intentions and in the process assure it of detailed intelligence of the enemy's concentration, disposition and movement, work for which Stuart, with his sharp eye for numbers and direction and his feel for terrain, seemed born; but he was headstrong too, not insubordinate but incurably theatrical, what with his plumes and capes and jingling spurs and incessant banjo music, and inclined thus, unless watched, to seek out foolhardy feats, long profitless rides around whole Union armies, for example, or raids netting nothing—boys' stunts, full of spirit and fun but better at enhancing Stuart's romantic vanity, Lee suspected, than at bolstering the survival of the Army of Northern Virginia. Oh, he'd done well enough when the march began, covering them with an elaborate screen as they crossed the Rappahannock and brilliantly fighting off a surprise Union cavalry assault at Brandy Station, and afterward, in a series of skirmishes at Middleburg and Upperville, he'd kicked so much sand in enemy eyes that Lee felt confident—for the moment, at least—that the main thrust of his campaign must still be secret; but then, restless as always and afire with success, Stuart asked to ride his corps off eastward to scout the distant Union rear, above Fredericksburg, and in a moment of folly Lee'd agreed.

Now came the consequences, for in Stuart's absence—and, worse, in his silence—he knew no more of the enemy's strength or movement than the immediate moment revealed. He'd urged caution, to be sure, had stressed prudence and vigilance and the necessity for undeviating attention to Yankee designs: "Be watchful and circumspect in all your movements," he'd warned, adding the instruction that at the first hint of a Union swing north Stuart must recross the Potomac and anchor his troopers on Lee's right flank, must not only screen Ewell's northerly thrust and Hill's and Longstreet's east but keep them abreast, hour by hour, of the Federals' location and direction. But that was like forbidding a nightingale to sing, alas, and now Stuart was gone, God knew where or to what fate, and without him Lee felt himself staggering, like a sightless cripple, across the *terra incognita* of rural Pennsylvania.

In ignorance lay disaster, he knew, and surprise led to panic, and he feared both more than he dared confess aloud; whereupon on Sunday night in Chambersburg, as if the lack of intelligence from Stuart weren't problem enough, he'd been dealt news so shocking the hated chest pain returned like a fury. A spy came in, a man Longstreet had sent behind Yankee lines weeks before to scout things out, and though Lee found the fellow shifty and disheveled and disliked dealing with him at all, he had to heed his tale: that the Union had two infantry corps in Frederick, scarcely half a day south, and was moving another two north.

His movements were known, then, the armies were closing, and presently, as surely as the sun rises and sets, they must collide. Where, though? Upon what ground and under what conditions? He must bring in Ewell, of course, and had sent forth orders summoning him back, southeasterly, so as to concentrate most effectively the full force of the Army of Northern Virginia; yes, and then . . . but then *what?* Without Stuart to give him some notion of the strength the Union was mustering against him—

He left the thought hanging and, pulling Traveller off the road, dismounted and stood for a moment beside him watching the long dusty column of raw Southern boys move on past through the humid afternoon. That their blood must soon stain this handsome countryside of pleasant farms and prosperous people now seemed inevitable; and—for he could no longer deceive himself of the cost of battle—many must remain behind forever. . . . Well, he had not wanted this war, fought it now only in defense of his beloved Virginia: but if fight here they must, or hereabouts, he must for his part deal the Union such a wound as would end the thing once and for all.

He rested in the shade, a map of Pennsylvania meticulously done by Jackson spread open across his knee, a tired gray man wondering where the week would end. Heat lightning flashed in the east; a moment later he heard, far off, the rumble of the thunder. Cashtown lay ahead, beyond South Mountain, and Ewell's march should bring a juncture near Mummasburg, a few miles past; then all the roads joined, like spokes coming together at the hub of a wheel, a brief distance further still, at the small market town labeled Gettysburg.

He was nineteen and hungry, but mostly his feet hurt. Back home on his father's hardscrabble farm in North Carolina they'd sometimes gone close to the ribs when times were tight, when the tobacco crop fetched less cash than they'd hoped for and the food laid by the summer before began to give out before the new garden came in, but they'd always scraped through—and, except in hot weather, when he'd wanted to, he'd never gone shoeless in his life.

No longer. Now his gut rumbled its emptiness and his feet were dirty and swollen and even bleeding in places. Well, no wonder. He and the rest, however many thousands of them there were, had marched all the way up here into Pennsylvania from the familiar landscapes of Virginia, day in and day out, a long dusty line stretching forwards and rearwards as far as the eye could see, and by the time they'd entered Maryland what little was left of his only pair of shoes was nothing but uppers, and not much of them. He'd tried wrapping his shoes, but the rags wore out too; and then he and his friends, all but a couple by then barefoot too, had taken turns wearing the few wearable pairs that remained. That helped, an hour here or there, but a decent pair of shoes would help more.

He soaked his feet in the branch alongside which they'd halted for the evening. That helped too, as did just lying there on the bank and not moving at all, the way he'd used to do when he went fishing; and afterward he and the rest made what supper they could from what cornmeal was left. A nice ripe tomato would've been nice, though, or some beans, or a fat old hare to roast over the fire. He wished he'd see one. North Carolina had lots.

Still, here he was, in Pennsylvania somewhere, and he'd might as well make the best of it—so the Captain said, anyway, and the Captain must take his orders from General Lee. Fair enough, but it was a long way from North Carolina, and when he'd lined up and signed up two years ago he'd thought it was to fight there, to defend his home, maybe even to defend Virginia, not walk all the way to Pennsylvania. . . . But he had, he had, and he'd fought at the Seven Days and Antietam and Fredericksburg and Chancellorsville too, and pretty soon now, there or someplace, he guessed he'd have to fight again.

Meantime his feet hurt, and when one of the sergeants came down the line with the rumor that a whole warehouse of shoes lay waiting in the town up ahead he perked up fast.

1

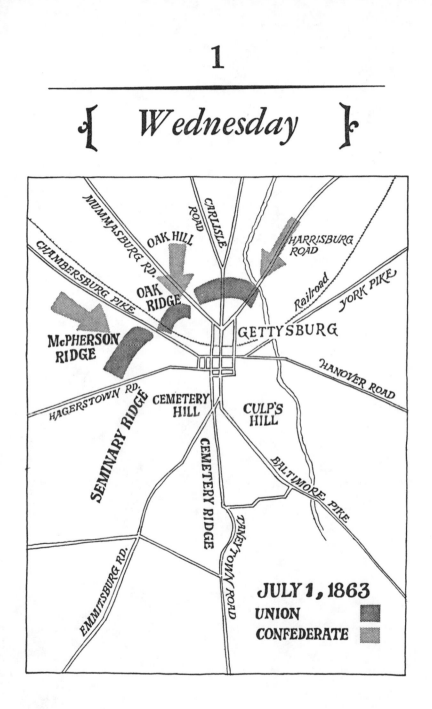

HISTORY OFTEN HINGES ON TRIVIA. Major General Harry Heth's division of Hill's corps, some five thousand footsore soldiers at most, held the eastward point of Lee's army this hot July morning; and a rumor they'd caught the day before, foraging further east still, had them restless to press on. The week earlier, so it went, the troops of General Jubal Early's division had gone through Gettysburg so fast, bound for York and that elusive double envelopment Lee hoped for, they'd missed a huge supply of shoes stored somewhere thereabouts . . . still there too, people claimed, and up for grabs by whoever moved soonest to seize them.

Heth vowed to move soonest. His men were as good as the best, if not better, wiry farm lads from North Carolina, Alabama, Mississippi and Tennessee, a few even from Virginia, but they'd marched more than two hundred miles over roads as rough as they were dusty and what shoes were left amongst them were ragged assemblages of pads and thongs that would fall apart tomorrow if they survived today. But if he could get on into Gettysburg—

He was off at daybreak, Archer's brigade out front probing and testing the pike into town, for skirmishers from Pettigrew's brigade had sighted a handful of Union troopers ranged along a creek bank nearby the afternoon before; but he expected little real resistance. Hill guessed the bluecoats were cavalry, probably no more than an observation detachment that would ride off if challenged, and he guessed Hill was right.

Both were wrong, though, and on both predictions: the Yankee cavalry was far larger than a detachment and instead of running it stood. Just before eight Archer's advance ranks crossed a rise of ground rumpling the pike and came abruptly under a fusillade of rifle fire from the banks of a stream ahead and below, where the figures of the bluecoats awaiting their arrival scurried left and right beneath the rising smoke. They halted at that, kneeling to rest and take stock for a moment, but the Federals gave them no more than a moment; from a second ridge beyond the creek bed, less than a mile to their front, and behind and above the riflemen whose firing had started it all, a Union battery began dropping a murderous cascade of cannon shot among them, thinning their numbers and disrupting their formation before they'd had a chance to claim their ground.

Yet to prolong their exposure would be fatal, so Archer moved them forward, down the slope, shaking them out into three lines of skirmishers as they went, and then Heth, who'd come up himself at the sound of gun-fire, called for Davis's Mississippi brigade and flung its infantrymen out in similar fashion to their left, the far north side of the pike; and it was thus, two brigades wide with their muskets extended, bayonets fixed, that they swept down the hill and into the valley below through the golden waves of ripening wheat, while eastward, ahead, the morning sun threw the Federal gunners into ornamental silhouette against the ridgeline. Then smoke obscured both sun and men, and somewhere—perhaps in the village of Gettysburg itself—a bell began to peal the hour . . . or maybe toll, for the day was to have gone differently from this.

It went as it would, however, an accident, a collision in the darkness of ignorance and miscalculation, and by now its chance beginning had set in motion a cruel, remorseless logic of man, moment and circumstance beyond the comprehension or control of either army. Heth's men poured down the eastern slope of the ridge, the first lines of skirmishers quickly followed by the main bodies of the brigades, halting to fire and reload as they went, Archer's along the line of the pike itself, Davis's across it and swinging north, like a gate, as they sought to take the bluecoats by flank; but though the advance proceeded, the Yanks' return fire seemed unusually heavy and they gave ground only slowly, nor—despite what appeared to be far fewer numbers—did they show they were feeling their losses, for their musketry remained as steady as ever. Repeating carbines, perhaps, getting off twenty rounds a minute to their own slow muzzle-loading four, if that. . . .

A fence slowed them before they made the creek-bed, but only briefly, and then they were splashing across and up the slope ahead, where the Yanks had withdrawn; whereupon—like a crash of lightning—they were struck by such a volley of rifle fire their first ranks went sprawling to the ground, bloody and twitching. At that and the volley succeeding it, their commanders waved them back, back down the ridge and across the creek and back up the hill they'd just descended, but there too they were hurt, and badly, for the fence stopped them altogether this time, clumping them like helpless puppies along its lower eastern edge and exposing them not only to the unrelenting fire from the hill but also to a surprise flanking attack out of the woods to their right. Many fell or were captured, and Archer himself was among them, the first of Lee's generals to be taken prisoner.

Davis's men did better beyond the pike, though, pushing on into the valley and gaining speed as they went, then—with the bulk of the Mississippians forging in behind the North Carolinians whose energy and dash had given the attack its momentum—crossing the creek double-time and sweeping up the ridge and across its crest after the Yankees, whose initial careful withdrawal now resembled a rout. A new valley lay ahead, perhaps a quarter of a mile across, with still a third long ridge beyond it. They moved down in good order, ranks aligned, muskets forward, many taking the natural path afforded them by a deep unfinished railroad cut, running forward precisely along their own route of march, whose steeply sloped banks seemed to offer almost perfect protection for their swift advance eastward upon the Federal rear; but that was to prove disastrous too, like the fence line that a little earlier had disrupted Archer's retreat, for as the cut filled and became congested, what appeared to be the entire Union army loomed suddenly upon its parapets, repeating rifles aimed menacingly into their midst, ordering them to throw down their muskets and surrender.

Most did, weapons clattering to their feet on the spot, and most of the few who did not—turning tail to run back out of the cut the way they'd come—were dropped in their tracks, and by noon what remained of Davis's brigade was coursing rearward across the ridge and the creek and up the long slope of wheat to the safety of their original position; but it was at frightful cost, for the abrupt reversal of their fortunes had left their numbers halved, and the half remaining was too shaken to rally.

II

Thus, with a rush and a rout, it began, and thus too, in a standoff by which neither army had advanced or improved its position, it might have ended; but history was set upon a more tragic course. A lull fell upon the field after Davis's withdrawal, and in it, the midday sun pouring mercilessly upon them, both sides paused to assess their losses and await events. By now—though certain of little more—Lee's men knew they faced a Union force larger and stronger than they'd suspected was in Pennsylvania at all; that it was heavily armed and ably led was apparent from the spirit with which it had defended itself. These were better soldiers than the bluecoats they'd whipped at Fredericksburg and Chancellorsville, tougher and stubborner and slower to give ground, and—though their own gift for attack undeniably had carried them to victory against superior numbers again and again—this time a certain prudence might well prove wise.

But the time was denied them. As they licked their wounds and awaited the arrival and instructions of Lee, riding toward them from Cashtown, a rapid succession of shell bursts exploding within the Union lines turned their heads left, to the north, where to their astonishment they could make out, a mile away across the pastures on the high ground where the ridges merged, a battery of Confederate artillery, and then another and another, hauling up their pieces and commencing fire on the exposed Federal flank . . . Ewell's corps, surely, run in from Carlisle as Lee'd ordered and entering the fray at a critical moment; whereupon, as the cannonade died, three brigades of butternut infantry came out of the woods on the hilltop and started forward for the Yankee right.

Their attack ended in but a third disaster, however. Only Iverson's center brigade lasted out the march, one of its companion units fumbling and stumbling and being halted at the outset, the other swinging wide of the line as it attempted to wheel; and Iverson's soldiers were almost annihilated halfway down the slope when a line of Yankee skirmishers, their presence missed in the haste and lack of reconnaissance with which the strike had been initiated, stood up from behind a stone wall angled to their flank and poured volley after volley point-blank into their ranks. Half went down at once, perhaps more, the survivors tripping across their fallen or falling bodies as they came forward, and then they too were on the ground, pinned, immovable, waving handkerchiefs or rags to signal their wish to surrender or else struggling to crawl their way backward to the security of the rear.

Lee saw it all, reaching the field to the swelling of gunfire that told him the morning's skirmishes were expanding into an engagement larger than he was prepared—at least yet—to fight. Taking a high point of the ridge where the clash had occurred hours earlier, he swept the scene with his glasses but was able to draw from it little reassurance. Attacks by his men had failed to his front and were failing even now to his left, and the Union seemed to be gaining strength in both directions; while beyond the two ridges to the east, below the spires and cupolas of the town, he could see line after line of blue-coats, brought on from some point south or east, streaming toward him through the streets of Gettysburg to reinforce its defenders. He slapped his gloves, stamped a foot. What forces were out there? What hornet's nest had he burst? Where was Stuart?

Choices remained, but none present satisfied him. To withdraw behind the mountains would keep his army intact, to be sure, but at the cost of nullifying its invasive potential; and though audacity was his hallmark, he'd invariably ensured its past expression with some such additional advantage as detailed knowledge of the enemy's placement and strength, superior position or surprise, so that to attack blindly now, knowing nothing of what lay before him, was to risk a general engagement for which his forces, though gathering rapidly, were still insufficiently concentrated. Yet to stand and wait was dangerous too, for even a cursory study of Jackson's map showed that the numerous roads into Gettysburg offered abundant means of reinforcing the Federal troops already there, as what he'd seen through his glasses confirmed; the longer he hesitated the less confidently could he hope to retain either superiority of numbers or flexibility of movement.

His chest ached with the stress of indecision. Such caution was unfamiliar, unpleasant, almost unnatural; yet reason argued and Longstreet urged it, for it was the latter's view—had been his view from the first days of planning back in Virginia—that though Lee's proposal to take the war to enemy territory was promising enough, its chances of success would be enhanced immensely by so maneuvering the Federals as to force them to attack on such ground and under such conditions as Lee himself chose: an offensive strategy, in short, but pursued with defensive tactics: make the Union fight on Confederate terms. . . .

Well, perhaps, perhaps. Meanwhile what must he do with the terms at hand?

Again, though, events intervened. Up the slope to his left, an hour earlier the scene of the Yanks' devastating enfilade from behind the stone wall, the soldiers of Ewell's corps had regathered and regrouped; and now, as Lee watched, they surged forward anew, but this time with such force and order as to resemble a great wave sweeping the field. They stormed the wall first, sending its defenders packing, then wheeled and plunged on south and east where their own left flank was marching to join them. At almost the same moment Lee caught the sound of additional firing from further east still, and as he raised his glasses he saw an immense contingent of fresh Confederate infantry pouring onto the field to attack the Union far right . . . the hand of Providence, he told himself, or at least the ferocity of Jubal Early, just in from York, and he waved Hill to send forward his own divisions against the Federals to their front.

A Cannae it might be, then, another Chancellorsville, if they moved swiftly and decisively to exploit its lucky logic: for by some happy coincidence his orders to concentrate had brought each element of his army into ideal position at the same instant. The divisions of Ewell's corps, Rode's men and Early's, were pushing the Yank right southward from the rising ground north of Gettysburg, while Hill's divisions, Heth's troops and Pender's, were up in strength now and ready to renew full-scale the assault on the Union left their skirmishers had failed to carry that morning; and Longstreet, stalwart Longstreet, stood stolid in reserve. The terms of battle had changed abruptly, therefore. He held the enemy in a giant claw; what remained was to close its grip.

III

That proved task enough. Though by midafternoon the Yanks were giving way all along the crescent of their defense, it was only after savage fighting on both sides and with casualties to match. Ewell's troops had the easier of it, perhaps, for after their initial reverses the men of Rodes's division made steady progress pushing the Federals south along the ridge from which they'd fought since noon; while Early's infantrymen, striking brutally at the Union far right, just north and slightly east of Gettysburg itself, found their advance going faster and faster as the lines before them began to slacken and at last to collapse altogether, single soldiers and then entire units abandoning their positions to turn tail and run like hares flushed from cover before the onrushing butternut tide.

Along the pike back to Chambersburg, though, the Yanks withdrew more stubbornly. Heth's men took at last the slope at which they'd balked that morning, but to heavy cost. The hundreds of Union troops holding it would let go only when they themselves could no longer stand, and their Confederate attackers paid almost as dearly. Heth himself fell, of a head wound, and Pettigrew's North Carolinians suffered such fearful losses some units emerged the far side of the ridge bereft of leaders or led, mere numbers on a roster that no longer existed; and through to their south, below the pike, Pender's soldiers were able to give the final eastward push that sent the bluecoats into rout, they too found it a harsh, bloody thing of load and fire and then run forward to slash and stab with the bayonet before halting, heart pounding, breath short, the dangerous span of seconds it took to reload and set off again—vicious going, every inch of it, and no glory anywhere.

Yet success it had aplenty—narrowly won, perhaps, but abundant in yield—and as Lee rode forward behind the accelerating advance of Hill's division, the great victory he had envisioned and maneuvered to effect seemed suddenly, by one of those turns of fate more common to war than his firm Christian faith preferred to admit, within his grasp. By then he had reached the grounds of a Lutheran seminary overlooking the town from a north-south ridge only recently cleared of Union defenders, and ahead of him, less than half a mile further east, the streets of Gettysburg teemed to the point of choking with the thousands of bluecoats, a few of them riding but most on foot, retreating before the force of his army's momentum; and where the two streams converged from north and west at the town square, rout was giving way to panic. Everything his glasses revealed told him the Union defense was collapsing in catastrophic disorder, was at least for the moment more mob than army, and that if he but *pressed*—

Hill joined him now, still pale and weak from an intestinal upset from which he'd only just risen, and concurred at once. Though the evidence of their eyes was enough, quick reference to maps hurriedly brought up by staff engineers confirmed Lee's assessment that the power of his double assault had forced the Federals into a funnel from which escape grew more difficult as their retreating numbers swelled: clogging Gettysburg itself, threatened equally from west, north and northeast, they had nowhere to flee but south, and the route there would be rocky—a pair of steep rocky hills, in fact, arising abruptly less than half a mile below the center of town.

They had names too, the maps showed, Culp's Hill to the east, Cemetery Hill nearer by, but what the topography made mandatory and urgent was that they be taken and cleared promptly, at once, before the day's offensive slackened its pace or spent its energy; for the hills and ridge connecting them, as well as the long ridge snaking south from Cemetery Hill, formed a natural defensive bastion, high, partly wooded and strewn with protective boulders, from which, if allowed to make a stand there and dig themselves in, the Federals would be troublesome to dislodge, while the roads to their rear, to Baltimore and Washington, must simplify their steady reinforcement. Immediately, then, they must be driven:

driven on, driven off, their rout made complete. So would Hill please—

But Hill wouldn't, regretfully. Oh, he accepted Lee's logic, saw the ground and the situation and the need to pursue their advantage; but his own men were exhausted and demoralized from the savagery of their many hours of fighting, needed time to catch their breath, patch their wounds, grab a meal, grab a nap—his corps had borne the brunt of the action, after all, had been engaged without pause since dawn, had suffered grievous losses from which it wanted some small opportunity to recuperate. . . . And Longstreet's corps was still back, near Cashtown, thus still hours from the field. His options narrowing, Lee shook his head, sighed, wondered again about Stuart; where *was* he? Then he turned and summoned a courier to ride word to Ewell to carry Cemetery Hill if he possibly could.

He must "press those people," Lee said, pointing, and soon—and asked himself privately how many they were.

He was still awaiting the first sounds of Ewell's attack when, the afternoon waning, Longstreet arrived, ahead of his troops, to make his own appraisal of the ground and its possibilities. Immense of chest and thigh, he had the deliberate air of a big man too, slower than Hill to act but more thoughtful when he did, and Lee was pleased and reassured to have him near, as much for his stolid calm and confidence as for his keen and seasoned eye for terrain. Presently, after a perfunctory greeting to them both, Longstreet was repeating with his own glasses the sweep Lee'd made earlier of the field before them, referring again and again to the map as he located this landmark or that; whereupon, his reconnaissance done, he looked up with a smile and pronounced himself de-delighted: though unarguably the accident of collision seemed to have chosen the battle site, as Lee complained, they could hardly ask better.

Lee was uneasy but listened. Just below Gettysburg proper, Longstreet explained, his fingers moving back and forth between map and landscape, the complex of Culp's and Cemetery hills and the saddle joining them leveled out to form a low ridge undulating its way two miles due south to end at last in a visible pair of steeper, more conical hills the map called the Round Tops. The Federal defense line along that sequence of natural features was thus like that of an inverted fishhook—with Culp's Hill the barb, Cemetery Hill the bend, the long ridge the shank, the Round Tops the eye—and since they themselves now pressed the Union all along the barb and bend, and by their presence along the parallel ridge could further press the shaft and eye as well, they had attained already an enveloping advantage; all that remained was to push the Yankee right, as Ewell was to do, while maneuvering around the Yankee left, as Longstreet proposed to do himself, hence threatening Washington and forcing the Federals into the folly of attack . . . *precisely* the fusion of offensive strategy and defensive tactics he'd urged all along.

Lee disagreed, emphatically, face reddening, for he

disliked equally the turn Longstreet's thinking had taken and the counsel it encouraged. His own aggressive martial style was uncomfortable with defensive fighting anyway, preferred initiative, preferred to push and press, but —more to the moment—he could scarcely imagine letting so pronounced an advantage as the day's successes had brought them go unexploited. Sit back and *wait?* "No," he said, and pointed to the hills and ridge ahead. "The enemy is there, and I intend to attack him there."

Longstreet said carefully, "If he's there it's because he's anxious to have us attack him there—good reason, it seems to me, not to do so."

Lee smiled wanly. . . . Old Pete: always stubborn, always cautious; in the end he'd come 'round. "No," he said a second time, firmly but a shade more gently, "he's there in position, and I'm going to whip him or he's going to whip me," wherewith, as Lee'd known he would, Longstreet let it go.

Yet Lee remained unsettled. His chest was tight; he felt vaguely threatened, oppressed; the euphoria he usually experienced at the prospect of triumph was absent. Though the swiftness of their afternoon advance had carried them to excellent position, how long could he hold it if the Federals rallied? What reinforcements must be heading toward them from Washington? His best hope lay in striking *again,* striking *now,* before Union strength matched—or exceeded—his own. Where was Stuart to tell him what was happening over there? Why had Ewell still not attacked?

He was fretting, uncharacteristically, but within a few minutes more he had his answer, or an answer of sorts: a courier from Ewell, crossing his own going the other way, reported Rodes and Early prepared to assault Cemetery Hill, as Lee wished, but only if . . . *If?* If *what?* If Lee could assure them of a simultaneous attack from the west, the courier replied for Ewell, so as to heighten the pressure. But Hill's corps was exhausted and unable to fight further today, Lee told him, and Longstreet's was still en route to Gettysburg; Ewell must go it alone if he possibly could. Then he turned again to Longstreet, who'd been watching the swift concentration of Union defenses up Cemetery Hill—they were digging in effectively, he reported, and being reinforced steadily from the rear, so if Lee were going to attack, though he himself believed attack mistaken, the sooner the better.

By now Lee's apprehensions were nearing despair—without Jackson, it seemed, nothing quite went right—but his spirits rose when two of Stuart's troopers came dashing in with an excited if confusing report of a long ride around the Union army, the capture of a mule train of more than a hundred Yank supply wagons laden with all manner of provender, hundreds of bluecoat prisoners, a skirmish at Hanover and a final hard gallop into Carlisle, thirty miles north, where the main cavalry body now waited. Lee was exasperated but relieved—Stuart was a scamp, but at least he'd kept his corps intact—and sent them back to fetch their companions. . . . He slapped his gloves, shot Longstreet a brief smile; perhaps it was still not too late.

IV

———————————————

Or was it? By now the sun was beginning to set behind South Mountain and, despite two sets of instructions urging action, Ewell's attack on Cemetery Hill had yet to begin, while across the length and breadth of the battleground, except for sporadic musket fire, the guns had fallen silent. Lee could wait politely no longer: the thing must be done, done now. So he remounted Traveller, nudged his flank and trotted off to find Ewell to tell him so.

That was easier intended than accomplished, however. At fifty-six he believed he'd seen the worst war could inflict—Mexico, Indian skirmishes out West, the last two years—and nothing would ever erase from his memory the bloodiness of that awful day on Antietam Creek, but what he encountered as he made his slow way through Gettysburg turned his ruddy face ashen. Both armies had left the townspeople and their homes and stores alone, scrupulously, but they'd brutalized each other with an abandon nearer hysteria than necessity. The streets were a chaos of bodies, Confederate and Union casualties heaped together all anywise, survivors crying for water and help while soldiers still on their feet pounded noisily past them in flight or pursuit. Little clumps of bluecoats still struggled here and there to escape to the safety of the hill ahead, but most left behind were prisoners, herded miserably into side streets and hustled at musketpoint to the rear; while his own gaunt men, ragged and dirty, shoved on the other way, blank, blind eyes seeing nothing, to the firing line assembling at the foot of the slope. What chilled him deepest, though, was the unearthly sound coming at him from every side, a high keening whine like the howl of a wolf, that he realized finally was the moaning of the wounded. His hands tightened on the reins; reflexively he spurred Traveller on, to speed his escape. This must once have been a pleasant, peaceable town of small civilized amenities—not a grand place of handsome mansions, lawns and vistas like the plantation country of Tidewater Virginia, of course, but tidy, friendly, its small stone, brick and frame cottages snuggling down flush with the streets, the sort of modestly comfortable village, prosperous, neighborly, churchgoing and decent, that was typical of the old America he'd known before the war—but no longer, no more, and on his head be the curse; he and Meade over there, wherever he was, had made it a charnel house.

Meade. George Gordon Meade: an old acquaintance in the fraternity of West Point and the tiny army they'd both served in the decades before Fort Sumter, now—and for the last several days, it appeared—commanding general of the Army of the Potomac and thus the antagonist he must best to win the battle at hand. Until he reached Chambersburg he'd expected to face Hooker, whom he'd whipped at Chancellorsville, and since Hooker's oversights and miscalculations were by now as familiar to him as McClellan's delays and Burnside's blunders, he'd anticipated the meeting with relish; but that hope faded with the spy's report that Hooker was out, Meade in. . . . Another of Lincoln's endless attempts to find the Union a winning general, Lee supposed, and welcome news to his own subordinates because it meant they faced an inexperienced and presumably lackluster foe yet again. For himself he was less sanguine: sooner or later, if only by chance, Lincoln must come upon a general who knew his business; meanwhile Meade, a cautious man, would make no mistake.

Ewell might, though—might dawdle, might balk—and to prevent his doing so was now paramount. Back in the valley he'd seemed Jackson reborn, fighting so fiercely and well at Winchester, he'd revived for a moment the aggressive spirit Lee'd feared lost with Jackson's death; but today . . . Lee rode slowly on, in search of him, and as he passed, his soldiers halted and parted to let him through, lifting their hats, so near exhaustion they tottered as they moved. Yet they were rekindled, it appeared, by his presence; a mystery, Lee thought, raising his own hat in return, and by no means the only one—in what other war would the women of a conquered village beg the autograph of their conqueror?

"You want the autograph of a rebel?" he asked one who did, surprised but amused—amidst all this devastation!

"I'm a true Union woman," she said, "but I do."

He nodded, halfway understanding, and signed and moved on, through Gettysburg's center square and then north, past the college, towards Carlisle. Here again the traffic was heavy in both directions, Confederate infantry streaming against him into town, Federal prisoners, nearly as numerous, moving in clumsy clumps for the rear, sullen, disgusted at themselves; and guns were coming up too—for storming Cemetery Hill, he hoped. At last, a mile or so above town, he found Ewell sitting with Rodes in an arbor behind a little house close by the pike, Ewell joking that he'd taken a sharpshooter's ball during the afternoon advance but emerged uninjured.

"It don't hurt at all to be shot in a wooden leg," he said, showing the hole, and they all laughed at that.

It was as well they did, too, for otherwise Lee found little to please him. Ewell's splendid advance from north and northeast, under Rodes and Early, seemed now to have stalled altogether; and Ewell himself, though jovial enough, seemed unable to rediscover the will to rise and move forward again to deliver the final, killing blow on Cemetery Hill—seemed indeed, like Longstreet, to have become preoccupied with defense. Patient but dubious, Lee heard him out with his accustomed courtesy. Rodes had done well, true, but his losses were terrible. Early's intervention had been equally successful, but he'd had to protect his left flank at a crucial moment, thus diluting his strength. Johnson's division had only now reached the field after a forced march of twenty-five miles and needed rest and food before undertaking a fresh offensive. Besides, Lee's instructions were ambiguous: he'd ordered Cemetery Hill attacked only if "practicable"—that was the word: "practicable," if the situation so indicated—and he, Ewell, took that to mean he was free to exercise his own discretion. And besides that, their position, though dangerous as a point from which to attack, was ideal to defend. . . .

Besides, besides, besides—Lee knew it could go on forever, this thing of finding reasons not to do what manifestly needed doing, and with a weary wave of his hand, though still smiling as politely as he could, he turned the rest aside. . . . Jackson was dead, to be sure.

Yet a new day loomed, a fresh chance, and if they could but act quickly enough after dawn, matters might yet go as he'd conceived; and when Early strode in a moment later, Lee put them all three the crucial question: "Can't you, with your corps, attack on this flank tomorrow?"

Well, maybe so, maybe not. . . . Rather than Ewell it was Early who answered, dark, dyspeptic, sour, splenetic, the most unpopular figure in either army, and what he had to say, ticking off arguments against his fingers like the prosecutor he'd once been, only deepened Lee's gloom. The approaches to Cemetery Hill were most difficult, to begin with. Meade was bound to concentrate there overnight and would be waiting, reinforced, for an attack up its rocky slopes. Casualties must be high. To the south, though, down at the Round Tops—*there* lay ideal ground for a fresh offensive: where Federal defenses were still weak, where by plunging ahead Lee could turn the Union left and—

"Then perhaps I'd better draw you around to our right," Lee put in. "Our line's already long and thin, and if you remain here the enemy may come down and break through."

Again Early disagreed. For his men to abandon terrain they'd just won would rob them of an important accomplishment; nor should he be expected to move his wounded so soon. No, no—and at this Ewell and Rodes nodded their concurrence—let Lee attack on the right tomorrow and he could rest assured they'd hold fast on the left.

Lee listened, head bent, and sighed again when they'd finished, disliking their counsel but unwilling to overrule their greater familiarity with the field and the capabilities of their own men. Early was able, besides, smart and combative both, and though his manner was coarse his judgment was excellent. So . . . Hill was battered and Ewell had balked. "Very well," he said, and rose, "It must be Longstreet," and thought suddenly how *slow* Longstreet was.

V

Necessity could be cruel; still, there it was—attack promptly or accept the likelihood of facing a reinforced Union army vastly larger than his own—and as he rode back west toward Seminary Ridge the choice of Longstreet to do the job seemed unavoidable. Yet he had no sooner taken up headquarters for the night alongside the Chambersburg Pike than his chest tightened and grew heavy again; doubt fluttered his stomach, loosened his gut. His options were so *few!* Except for Pickett's division, his infantry was now east of the mountains and could no longer safely withdraw. Perhaps a southerly maneuver to the right, around the Federal left, would indeed threaten Washington, as Longstreet counseled, but without Stuart's cavalry to scout and screen the way . . . And Ewell had funked. Attack it must be, then, before Meade had time to strengthen his defenses, and Longstreet it must be who must make it.

As insurance he would pull Ewell around toward the center, though, let Early object all he would, for his line —circumferential and exterior, whereas Meade's was interior altogether—was already imprudently long; and he sent Ewell revised orders to that effect. He'd scarcely done so, however—his simple supper of beans and cornbread went unfinished, though he held onto his tin cup of chicory—before Ewell himself came back, peg leg and all, huffing and puffing his readiness to reconsider. Johnson's reconnaissance had convinced them both, it now appeared, convinced Early too, that Culp's Hill could be taken tomorrow, thus Cemetery Hill along with it, which it flanked: so if Lee would please leave his divisions where they were, not shift them as proposed . . . why, then— harumph, harumph—he was prepared to attack in concert with Longstreet after all.

That changed everything, of course, and for the better; and in his delight at the restoration of Ewell's resolve, Lee beamed and chuckled and sent his favorite eccentric back to his men on a tide of affection and esteem. Then he turned to Longstreet and instructed him to attack on the right as soon, next morning, as he could. For thus it must go: Ewell assaulting Culp's and Cemetery hills, Longstreet the Round Tops, the two of them crushing the Federals caught midway along the ridge between like pecans in a nutcracker. Longstreet nodded his understanding but left his opinion unspoken, and presently, heavily, took his silent leave: sad, moody, like so many big men, something of a stoic—he'd lost three children to diphtheria last winter. Like Ewell he had much to do.

The field lay quiet. The moon was high and pale and bathed the countryside in a ghostly light, and beneath it, except where the pickets kept their fires, the armies slept . . . Lee too, at last, though it was a restless sleep punctuated with pain and broken by a dread whose source he could not establish; and finally, still weary, he rose and stepped outside, cloaked against the dew, to pace the night. Well, well: life held such ironies, for the Lees as for the rest—perhaps it was the punishment accorded pride. He'd made his plans and the plans were good, and somewhere he'd gone terribly wrong.

He finally found the field hospital in a shed behind one of the big houses on the main street bisecting the town north and south, but he'd known he must be near it it long before he got there. The keening cries of the wounded awaiting surgery were signal enough.

He'd seen them before, of course, but nothing as bad as this. The sergeant had given him and a friend the job of bringing in litter cases, and he'd agreed readily—it could just as soon be the other way around out there, and if his turn came, or when, he hoped someone else would be around to bring him in too. Meanwhile here they were, the big fellow between them gray with pain from a shattered leg, and the sooner the surgeon got to him the better.

But that was easier thought than accomplished. The shed, a long tin roof sloping downward from the side of a barn and supported at its two outer corners by rough log uprights, was thronged with casualties. They lay or sat on the ground, inside and out, in every imaginable condition, some obviously near death, others glassy-eyed with shock, and the air was ripe with the stench of blood. The center of activity, however, was near the middle of the interior, where beneath a single kerosene lamp hung from a beam in the roof the surgeon did his work.

He was a stocky, bearded fellow, sleeves rolled past his elbows, his apron dark with blood, and his hand held a saw. To his signal, litter-bearers brought forth this case or that to lie before him on a pair of rough pine planks laid between two sawhorses. Sometimes he swapped saw for knife, then branding iron, then back again. He hardly paused between patients. They came on steadily. There was no knowing from appearances why he chose one case over another—there was no waiting line, just a crowd, and it was his appraisal, at a glance, that said who should come next.

Whereupon, abruptly, they did. He gave them but a nod and they moved forward to roll their burden onto the table. He looked down swiftly, motioned to the orderly at his elbow to rip back the britches, and turned to his patient.

"Bite this," he said curtly, and to them, "Hold him down, now," and then, after giving his sweaty forehead a swipe with his elbow, he started to cut.

2

{ Thursday }

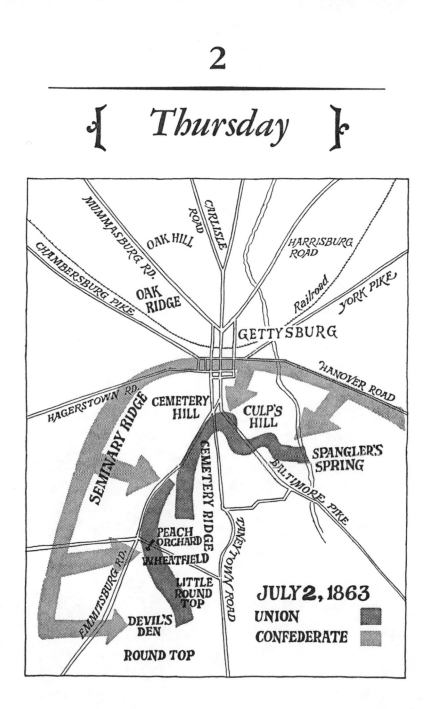

MUMMASBURG RD.

CARLISLE ROAD

OAK HILL

HARRISBURG ROAD

CHAMBERSBURG PIKE

OAK RIDGE

Railroad

YORK PIKE

GETTYSBURG

HANOVER ROAD

HAGERSTOWN RD.

SEMINARY RIDGE

CEMETERY HILL

CULP'S HILL

CEMETERY RIDGE

SPANGLER'S SPRING

BALTIMORE PIKE

PEACH ORCHARD

TANEYTOWN ROAD

WHEATFIELD

LITTLE ROUND TOP

EMMITSBURG RD.

DEVIL'S DEN

ROUND TOP

JULY 2, 1863
UNION
CONFEDERATE

HIS HANDS WERE TIED: it came to that: neither he nor Meade had chosen the field or initiated the action—geography, chance and the judgments of subordinates had done it for them—but now they both, and the thousands upon thousands of men of their respective armies, must make what they could of the consequences.

He would do his best, of course, as he always had, and thereafter, with King Harry at Agincourt, let God dispose the day; yet as he rode slowly south along Seminary Ridge, Lee felt unaccustomedly bereft of an instinct for the enemy's dispersal, strength and fatal weakness that had served him so well so often. To his left, across the gentle swale bisecting the open valley separating them by what looked to be three-quarters of a mile or so, Cemetery Ridge began to take form and color as the eastern sky grayed and whitened behind it; and as it did the shapes and bustle of the bluecoats going into position down its near slope came clear too—Yanks by the hundreds, his glasses showed, and more coming up steadily, while among and behind them guns were moving into place alongside. . . . It would be a bloody day.

His day, though, or his men's—they could do anything, after all—if they but struck incisively and soon; for though Meade might boast better defensive ground over there, the reinforcements he needed to bolster his strength must still be en route, and before they arrived Lee purposed to sever his army, left and right, then destroy each remaining segment piece by piece.

If, however, *if:* if Longstreet could overcome his constitutional slowness and send his divisions off promptly; if Ewell's nerve held and he launched his concerted attack at the first sound of Longstreet's guns; if Stuart's cavalry reached Gettysburg soon enough to enlarge Lee's intelligence and thereafter take a hand in the fighting.

Lee sighed; he seemed lately to be forever sighing. . . . Age, perhaps? Was he running down? Jackson had known no such word as *if,* no such doubt; had brooked no such delays and distractions; and now lay dead in Lexington, his genius, good counsel and inflexible strength dead with him.

Here instead, though, was Longstreet, coming up to have a look after his own—no doubt substantial—breakfast; and despite their apparent differences Lee immediately took heart, for this was a man whose firm purpose and stout loyalty he need never question: Old Pete, his warhorse, as dependable as Traveller. Behind him a moment afterward came Hill, face pale against his long red hair and beard, tense, drawn, still shaken from dysentery, then Harry Heth, head bandaged from his wounds of the day before, and last young John Bell Hood, fairest, tallest and most gallant of them all, Kentuckian by birth, Texan by choice, and already, scarcely into his thirties, the most aggressive division commander in Longstreet's corps . . . and—well, yes, truth to tell—a favorite of Lee's: a fine boy, a fighting boy, a boy whose future was as bright as any the Confederacy held.

It would be a council of war, then, though he had called none; so Lee began. His plan, he told them, was as he'd outlined it the evening before: Longstreet to take the right, down Seminary Ridge, and attack northeastward up the roadway diagonally crossing the valley between the ridges, thus taking the Federals on Cemetery Ridge on the flank; meanwhile Ewell, across the way, would initiate his attack on Culp's and Cemetery hills when—

"But the ridge is already heavily defended," Longstreet put in. Till now he'd sat quietly with Hood astride a snake-rail fence edging the woods, whittling at a stick of fallen timber while Lee spoke; on realizing his chief's continued intention to attack despite the night's obvious reinforcements, however, he tossed the stick aside, closed his knife and, dropping to the ground, said gruffly, "My God, they've been digging in over there the whole damn time. General, with all due respect, we'd be wiser to slip around to the right, get ourselves situated between the Yanks and Washington, then sit back in good order and make them attack us."

Lee waited a moment, face reddening as it always

did when his patience wore thin: Longstreet was a fine fighter and noble friend but no thinker, alas, and these repeated attempts to imagine grand Napoleonic strategies had become tiresome. "No, sir," he said, and turned to point with gloved hand across the valley. "The enemy is here, and if we do not whip him he'll whip us."

A tight, cold silence followed, Hill and Hood watching carefully as Lee and Longstreet eyed one another; but it ended without further acrimony when a staff engineer Lee'd sent south earlier to reconnoiter galloped in to report the lower end of Cemetery Ridge and both Round Tops still clear of Federals.

"No question?" Lee asked eagerly. "No hearsay? You got there?"

"And saw for myself, sir. From a spur on Little Round Top."

Lee's eyes gleamed his satisfaction. "You see, gentlemen," he said, clapping his hands and turning to take them all in, "Meade's still unprepared. The race now is to the swift. . . . Please begin your preparations," and signaled an aide to bring Traveller.

II

———————

Across town at Ewell's headquarters, however, his waxing spirits began once again to wane. Observation of Culp's and Cemetery hills from the cupola of an almshouse north of Gettysburg revealed them both impressively better defended, in strength and disposition of forces alike, than at sundown the night before; indeed, their steep, rocky slopes bristling with men and guns, they appeared now all but impregnable, and at the thought Lee felt anew that inner shudder of misgiving, unfamiliar but unmistakable, that for the last several days had so sapped his confidence. Meade had the advantage of him in position, unquestionably, with a shorter line to protect and interior routes of reinforcement and supply—which made this a propitious moment to reconsider, perhaps, to sit and await developments or even maneuver southward, as Longstreet urged; if not to withdraw altogether. . . .

But no, no indeed—he shook his head abruptly, impatiently—that was not his way at all: he was an aggressive general and his was an aggressive army, and by no other attitude could they hope, outmanned and outgunned and outfactoried as the Confederacy unarguably was, to defeat so powerful an enemy as Lincoln's massive Union. Wit, cunning, speed, above all *audacity*—such were his strengths and the strengths of the Army of Northern Virginia; he was not called The Gray Fox for nothing. *Press,* he urged Ewell, press hard, and by that pressure prevent Meade from turning to repel Longstreet on his flank.

Ewell nodded, though so absently Lee was uncertain whether to take it as assent or mere understanding; but it was not his way to belabor instructions, nor to make them unduly detailed—he expected his subordinates to work out their tactics for themselves, and Jackson, of course, had never needed more than his most general intentions to effect precisely appropriate battlefield designs. . . . Well, but Jackson was gone now, *gone,* a hard truth but God's will, so he must simply hope Ewell had inherited a portion of his gift with the lion's share of his command.

Back on Seminary Ridge a little later, however, he found fresh cause for discouragement. Hill's divisions were where he'd wanted them, south of the Chambersburg Pike and strung out along the eastern slope of the ridge in position to join and support Longstreet's support when it rolled that far north, but Longstreet's own divisions, those commanded by Hood and McLaws, had made no movement at all to take up their starting point well to the south; and when in his impatience he brusquely ordered Longstreet to set off at once it was only to receive a request for still further delay: one brigade had yet to reach the field, it seemed, and with George Pickett's division a day distant and unavailable until tomorrow—

Lee seethed, his face scarlet, realizing he had no choice but to agree, for it was undeniable that Longstreet's corps would need all the strength it could muster in the coming attack; yet the man's sheer *pokiness* was exasperating—worse, it was dangerous—and that estimate seemed confirmed by the news, nearing noon, that Federal signalmen were busily occupying lookouts all over the Round Tops. . . . Ah, well: Meade was no fool; sooner or later, given time, he was bound to extend his line southward to protect his left flank. Why give him time, though?

But that was spilt milk; the need now was to yield Meade no more, to move out and move on; and Lee took heart again when a few moments later, albeit tardily, Longstreet's powerful divisions began ponderously but surely to rise and group and set off south, in good spirits despite the harsh midday heat—they were his toughest, subbbornest fighters, after all, their strength and grit proven through a dozen campaigns, lean, leathery countrymen proud of their appetite for adversity and spurred by it to wage war even more ferociously. Like Longstreet they were slow, no question of that, but when they moved at last, they moved with a power denied suppler soldiers; commander and corps were alike in that, and no enemy facing them would escape a brutal contest.

Off they went, then, a force to reckon with, and then to Lee's dismay back they came, Longstreet himself fuming—enemy surveillance from the Round Tops held them in such plain view, he said gloomily, he must take a more circuitous route if they were to preserve the secrecy their flanking attack wanted, and that meant starting over by way of a protective valley cloaked by a ridge further west. Again Lee assented—for again he had no choice—but with the sinking sense that again he'd lost valuable time: the afternoon was advancing, with no one yet in place to begin the assault by which he hoped to turn the battle and with it the course of the war; and when word reached him that finally Hood's troops had reached the far right end of the line, three miles south, it was with the additional news that Yank skirmishers were there too, straight ahead, awaiting their advance in a peach orchard.

Even had he chosen to, it was too late to turn back; for already the guns had begun to roll down where Longstreet's assault was to open, while across town, where Ewell waited, firing had broken out too, and—as he'd ordered—at nearly the same moment. He was committed, for well or ill, along the outside of an arc more than five miles from north end to south; he could only hope Meade, defending the far shorter interior, was still below his potential strength.

Among Longstreet's division commanders, meanwhile, matters seemed less final. Discovering the massed ranks of bluecoats opposing them across the way, McLaws returned to argue that Lee's plan, however imaginative earlier, ought now to be modified: instead of catching the Federal flank, as intended, he'd be exposing his own. Moments afterward Hood reached a parallel conclusion half a mile further south: ahead of him the rocky warren of boulders called the Devil's Den, and beyond and above it the steep, stony slope of Little Round Top, not only teemed with defenders but offered awesome obstacles in themselves—to maneuver southward around the Round Tops and attack the true Federal flank and rear, as his scouts had just found still possible, was surely the wiser and more prudent course. . . .

Here Longstreet's proverbial stubbornness took a

fresh course of its own, however. Obdurate the night before and that morning in his conviction that the assault at hand was futile, possibly fatal, he stuck now to the letter of Lee's plan: he had not changed his mind, true, but he'd lost the argument and Lee'd overruled him, and his loyalty was absolute. "General Lee's orders are to attack up the Emmitsburg Road," he reminded them both; and with that ordered both off.

III

Thus at last it began, in disagreement and dissent, yet in good order too. Lee's plan called for Longstreet's corps to advance by echelon from right wing to left, each brigade of its two participating divisions stepping off one by one as the brigade to its right came abreast moving northeastward up the Emmitsburg Road, the intended effect being—if all went well—to garner momentum and power as the gray wave swept north. Law's brigade was first, the farthest right of Hood's division, but almost immediately his Alabamans were struck by a hail of musketry from the viny thickets and boulders of the Devil's Den, which offered limitless cover for sharpshooters, and a moment afterward Robertson's brigade of Texans plunged into the struggle there too, then two brigades of Georgians under Benning and Anderson, and the clash became as bloody as it was already confused. Among the caves and crevices and through the nearly impenetrable mazes of underbrush soldier fought soldier to the brink of hysteria: so close was the combat that lines and ranks vanished, and fields of fire with them, the men themselves firing from the ground and from behind rocks and trees like Indians, thereafter stumbling forward to club away at the enemy with emptied muskets. Then Hood fell, shot from his horse by a shell fragment in the arm, to be carried away on a litter, and with his departure what shard of order remained fell to the private discipline and loyalty of individual soldiers; yet somehow they held on, held together, recognizing one another as the smoke parted or lifted and forming ranks afresh, tentatively, roughly, and with no more conscious purpose than to re-establish the security of comradeship, to renew their push eastward against the forbidding slope of Little Round Top.

It was nearing five by now, with McLaws's division still unengaged, nor indeed any Confederate troops save Hood's, but around to the right of the Devil's Den a push of another sort had begun. Two regiments of infantry sent to the foot of Big Round Top to rid it of a nest of pesky sharpshooters had done the job, then moved on, up through the woods and around the boulders of the steep slope, to the top itself—where their commander suddenly found himself overlooking the entire battleground. Below him and scarcely half a mile north he could see the bald crown of Little Round Top and—more yet to the point—the fact that except for a few Yank signalmen it appeared hardly defended at all; and when, moments later, orders came from Law to take the lower hill at once he motioned his men to follow him and pushed on again, down into the forested valley between—where their ranks were bolstered by three regiments, Alabamans and Texans, who'd fought through the Devil's Den to that point— then up the south side of Little Round Top.

Things went smoothly for most of the way, too, with no Union resistance and no sign, for that matter, of prior Union presence; but abruptly, nearing the crest, that illusion ended with a burst of point-blank musket fire into their midst so concentrated and so deadly they had no choice but to hug the rocks and earth and hope for swift reinforcement. Then the musketry from the summit was enhanced by an infernal spray of canister from two artillery guns, again at little more than the range of a shotgun; and at that the young Confederate colonel knew he and his men had been cunningly outfoxed: they could neither safely retreat nor safely remain where they were. He shook out their line, then ordered them to charge.

Desperate, gallant and doomed, they did as he told them, rising to their feet and bounding like hares up the bare, bouldered hill, shrieking their country yells and brandishing their muskets, some firing from the hip as they ran, and for a moment their sheer audacity carried them on into the Union lines; but then the Yanks shook themselves out too, forming hard, tight defense perimeters that resisted penetration and closing ranks around their fallen so swiftly and neatly no weak spots remained. Behind them fresh contingents of bluecoats were sprinting into the action as well, troops unwearied from the long march and climb that by now were taking their toll of Confederate energies, and additional guns were being wheeled into place, then turned and fired head on into the attackers' ranks. Back and forth the line surged, blood standing in puddles on the rocks, and the litter of dead grew so great that soldiers of both sides fell to firing from behind and around the mounds of corpses; but at last the weight of the Federal defense—eight full regiments against the South's depleted five—combined with the essential folly of attacking against such hostile terrain to exact the inevitable turn of battle. . . . Then abruptly everything fell apart when a regiment on the far Yank left rose and came swooping downhill in a bayonet charge, and the exhausted Alabamans facing them turned tail and ran like a herd of wild cattle, stopping only at the foot of the slope when they were reinforced there by the survivors of the push through the Devil's Den; and there they stood, bloody, battered, fought out and worn out, piling up rocks as barricades to fire behind, to await the Yank counterattack that must come next. It never did, though, and the day ended for them like that; but they'd failed to take Little Round Top.

IV

———————

Meanwhile, if belatedly, they got some slight relief when the attack shifted to their left, where after another succession of delays ordered by Longstreet the brigades of McLaws's division had begun at last their share of Lee's proposed advance. From the first its daring was clear: facing them no more than half a mile northeastward across the Emmitsburg Road—and as visible as sheep in a Shenandoah Valley pasture—bluecoats thronged the little peach orchard and wheatfield beyond it they'd spotted earlier. They charged on over anyway, though, shouting and shrieking, Kershaw's South Carolinians in the lead, Longstreet himself walking out part of the way to wave and yell them off, then Semmes's Georgians and after them still another brigade from Georgia led by Wofford, all three making head on for a low stone wall edging the west end of the wheatfield. There they encountered a terrible hail of musketry, volley upon volley of fire so fierce and so continuous—for the Yanks had waited for them to come into range before shooting, and shot by echelon as well—they lost untold numbers straightaway, among them Semmes, shot dead as he struggled through the waving grain; yet they came on and came on, hard, mean, half-mad with the folly of their task, and for a few moments, though struggling bitterly to do it, they carried the field before them, pushing the Federals back and heading for Cemetery Ridge in the distance.

By then the fourth and last of McLaws's brigades was fighting in the peach orchard, Barksdale's Mississippians, soldiers famous throughout both armies for their viciousness in combat, tearing into and over the Federal guns posted between the trees, then turning—Barksdale himself in the lead, his long white hair sweeping his shoulders, sword raised—to join their comrades as they rushed for the Union lines up ahead.

They were no more destined to succeed, however, than Hood's men at the Round Tops. Undetected and apparently unsuspected by what little reconnaissance Lee's engineers had completed, a huge force of Union infantry and artillery had swung southward—again exploiting the advantage of Meade's short interior lines—to mass themselves against the eastern end of the valley, up the slope and along the crest of the ridge; and as Barksdale's savage fighters plunged toward them they held their fire until the last, then let loose point-blank, round after round, bringing the Mississippians down like wild turkeys in a field, and when some few still came on it was only to be swept down with equal brutality by the forty guns or more lining the ridge. Barksdale himself was one of them, chest blown out and both legs riddled, to bleed slowly to death in the valley, but he was only one: half of his command lay with and around him, dead, wounded, dying, mutilated, those still alive screaming or moaning or simply gurgling their anguish as the sun set and twilight descended.

The rest—those who'd survived more or less untouched—fell back to a line along a little stream halfway between the road and the ridge, neither victors nor vanquished, and with their retreat Longstreet's role in Lee's grand double assault ended in what could only be regarded as a standoff: for though he'd gained little more than half a mile of ground, and won neither Little Round Top nor Cemetery Ridge, he'd lost none either, and clearly, as he'd foreseen, against immensely superior numbers. . . . But men he'd lost aplenty, at least a third of those who'd gone forward, Semmes and Barksdale forever, Hood for any future worth thinking about; so his pride in what he'd done had to be tempered by his grief at what doing it had cost.

Lee could share that concern, and did, but for the moment he could give it no more than passing thought. Distressed at Longstreet's obvious failure to carry the right, though still unfamiliar with the details of the fighting there, he must hope now for more positive results from the remaining forces of his army as yet uncommitted; and from his command post near the center of Seminary Ridge he watched with mounting satisfaction as the assault moved closer to hand. Longstreet's last brigades being engaged, the momentum now passed—since he remained bound to the principle of attack by echelon— northward to the men of Hill's corps. They, at least, moved off without delay, and in good order and sequence, Wilcox's brigade of Alabamans first, heading straight for the line of ridge just north of the point at which Barksdale's Mississippians had been thrown back, then Lang's Floridians and Wright's Georgians, all three as tidily aligned as if on parade; and for its initial five or ten minutes their advance was beautiful to watch, for— as Lee's glasses showed him—they were marching in a fine, firm mass on the weakest spot in the Federal defense, a gap of both men and guns through which, with spirit and luck, they must surely pass, thus breaking the Union line and leaving its severed parts to be destroyed one by one. . . . On, then, he silently urged them; drive on, drive on.

But then things began to go wrong everywhere; it seemed that sort of day. The three brigades already launched were simply too few to complete the breakthrough he wanted, good beginning though they seemed to have made, yet the brigades supposed to follow them had failed to step off as scheduled. Posey's Mississippians and Mahone's Virginians were next in echelon, but because of some confusion about their orders neither was moving, nor was Pender's division, following them in line, which stalled when its commander was blown off his horse by a stray shell fragment; in the ensuing confusion his soldiers lost their momentum and his successor his nerve, so that the three brigades already closing on the ridge had to carry on without further support or replenishment. Yet for a few bright moments it seemed to them —as to Lee, watching them—they might still turn the tide. Wilcox's brigade plunged through the Yank skirmishers and on up the slope against a ferocious defense by a handful of bluecoats brandishing bayonets, and Lang came on too, close beside, while a quarter of a mile northward, to their left, Wright and his Georgians not only pierced the Federal line but swept past it to the crest of the ridge, there to end at last silhouetted against the twilight sky in full view of both armies. The entire Union rear lay un-covered before them.

A brief look was all they got, however. On both sides Yank infantry were bearing down, and behind them fresh Federal troops were moving swiftly to close their route of retreat. Suddenly all but surrounded, and with no hope of reinforcement from Lee, they turned and slugged their way back down the ridge and into the valley across which, only minutes before, they'd charged so brilliantly, leaving half their number dead, wounded or captured; when the smoke lifted they could see nothing but the corpses of the fallen. Sweaty, exhausted, bitter with the belief they'd had victory stolen from their grasp, they staggered back to the safety of Seminary Ridge. They'd given their best, perhaps more, and it was too little.

V

Nor was the remainder of the afternoon's action more successful. Throughout the long wait for Long-street to open his attack on the right, Lee'd awaited as well the sound of Ewell's guns on the left—diversionary in intent, but to be followed by a genuine assault on Culp's and Cemetery Hills if weaknesses opened—and the reassurance they'd afford that he'd be pressing Meade the length of his line. He waited till weary, however, hearing nothing from the direction of Gettysburg and the rolling land north and east of it but sounds of movement —men and horses, surely, no doubt guns and caissons too, but no rifle fire, no cannonade, no hint that the fighting he'd hoped for had begun. Meanwhile Stuart galloped in, the incomparable Jeb, ruddy, eyes twinkling an exuberance no one on Seminary Ridge any longer dared indulge, mouth smiling through his great curly beard, spurs jingling gaily as he strode forward, ever the boy, to report to his chief. . . . He'd had a bully grand ride, it seemed, all the way 'round the Union army, and—

"Here at last, general." Lee's eyes flashed, but his voice was icy and his interruption curt. "I've heard nothing from you in days, sir—*nothing*, sir; *days*, sir—and was depending on your eyes and ears."

Stuart's face abruptly fell; he was unaccustomed to even the suggestion of rebuke. "But I've brought you a hundred and twenty-five wagons and teams, general," he halfway stammered, a bright child dangling a toy to win a parent's approval, and ended lamely, "and all sorts of supplies. . . ."

"And all a burden to me now." Unpleasant, unpleasant, Lee thought: the air between them rippled with tension—whereupon, his anger quickly spent, he as quickly softened. "Well, well," he said, "we'll discuss this no longer. Help me fight these people," and sent Stuart off to bring in his cavalry. Bearing a grudge could be burdensome too; besides, the boy'd meant well, as boys do: he thought fleetingly of Custis and Rooney, his sons, boys themselves despite their generals' stars, and Rooney only recently wounded. . . .

By then, nonetheless, the uses to which cavalry might be put were few and those mostly futile, for the enemy was all too clearly located, the chance to maneuver had passed and the fighting had closed. With the failure of Longstreet's and Hill's troops to penetrate the Union left and center, moreover, it had shifted northward to Ewell, whose guns could be heard, at long last, from the direction of Culp's and Cemetery hills. Yet those welcome opening salvos were quickly answered and soon stilled by return fire of equal or greater force from Yank batteries snugly dug in and tightly fortified along the hilltop during the protracted interval—from twilight yesterday till sundown today—created by Ewell's hesitations; and by the time the three brigades of Johnson's division were sent in to launch the infantry attack on Culp's Hill, any hope of either surprise or advantage had vanished.

They forged forward anyway, the rising ground ahead darkening even as they came on, for a minute or two carrying the Federal skirmishers before them and sweeping smoothly up the steep slope, shrieking the battle cry that chilled the blood of all who heard it as they neared the wooded crest; but then, as had happened so often that day, they entered the range of the enemy's muskets and the slaughter began. Jones's Virginians found themselves pinned where they were, neither atop the hill nor in position to flee it, with Jones himself down, and their flanking companions, more Virginians under Williams, stepped into a similar trap a moment later, effectively removed from the fight almost as soon as they'd entered it. Still a third Virginia brigade, commanded by Steuart, made better progress to their far left by rounding the Union right and striking north up the hillside along row upon row of abandoned Yank trenches; but then they too were halted short of the summit by freshly dug fortifications of mounded earth and logs from behind which the hill's defenders were able to pour a nearly continuous volley of musketry into their quickly thinning ranks. Finally, after two hours of unbroken fire, both sides quit the fight as a standoff, settling into the darkness where they were, to the cries and moans of the wounded.

VI

Meanwhile Jubal Early's attack on nearby Cemetery Hill was meeting greater immediate success. Two of his infantry brigades—one from Louisiana under Hays, the other comprised of North Carolinians commanded by Avery—formed the first wave, storming pell-mell up the hillside against the three lines of bluecoats awaiting them. Though Avery himself went down almost at once, his men held their pace, heads ducked but muskets raised as they pierced and passed one Yank line after another, overshot enemy cannon and rifle fire sweeping like a fiery but harmless wind above them; while to their right Hays and his soldiers crossed in quick succession Federal defenses aligned first near the foot of the slope, then along a stone wall midway to the crest, finally in fresh rifle pits lodged snugly behind a mound of felled trees. Smoke covered what little the darkness had failed to conceal, and in the obscurity the Confederate attackers smashed and clubbed their way to hilltop, there to penetrate and at last to possess the bend of Meade's great fishhook. It was a signal triumph.

It was also brief. The foothold Hays had won was limited to the survivors of his and Avery's brigades and could scarcely be held unless promptly reinforced; and indeed Ewell's orders had directed Rodes to send his division forward and upward to support Early's as soon as the defenses ringing Cemetery Hill were breached, and Early himself had held back Gordon's Georgia brigade from the first attack to do the same thing. To Hays' horror no support came up, however, and to add to his sense that his position was precarious he could see almost nothing in the deepening gloom; so when a mass of men neared his in the dusk, he had his men hold their fire till certain they'd not fire on friends. His caution proved nearly suicidal. The newcomers were Federals and they were constrained by no such prudence, firing three volleys into Hays' ranks almost as soon as observed and shattering the Confederate perimeter so thoroughly Hays was left with little choice, lacking reinforcement or any hope now of getting it, but to call retreat and withdraw the tattered remnant of the two attacking brigades back down the hill they'd believed was theirs.

They got there with few further casualties, too, for the darkness had rendered fire from either side ineffective except when point-blank, and at the foot they were able to reorganize and shake out a fresh line of defense against a Yank counterattack. None came, though, and they remained in their rifle pits throughout the night, sleeping fitfully by their silent guns and muskets, their fallen companions crying for water and help on either side and the ripe reek of blood on the air, while behind them, in the shacks and barns and parlors of Gettysburg, the surgeons sawed and seared and their patients screamed. Meanwhile Culp's and Cemetery hills, like the Round Tops and Cemetery Ridge, remained clearly if shakily Yank.

Results of the day's assaults had been disappointing on every front, in fact, for despite the substantial incursions effected by Johnson and Hood at either end of the line, failure to support the penetrations achieved by Wright's and Hays' men had caused the virtual collapse of Lee's intended attack by echelon; though as he received the successive shamefaced reports of disaster back at his command post on Seminary Ridge, Lee himself betrayed no disruption of his habitual composure. Inwardly he was aboil with frustration and rage at its source, however, for it now seemed to him manifest that his subordinates were unable to employ wisely and aggressively the tactical discretion he customarily—and always, until now, successfully—gave them. Their soldiers could do anything, to be sure, but casualties the day before had totaled eight thousand, today seemed likely to run higher still, and neither they nor he could afford such subtractions unless certain of victory from them. Prudence, prudence, he counseled himself: disengage, withdraw, survive to fight another day. . . .

But he would not; could not. Meade was over there, hardly a mile away on the ridge opposite, and the issue between them must somehow be resolved, not left in the limbo to which these two hot days of inconclusive struggle had led. Nor was he without resources, after all: Stuart's cavalry was available, however tardily, and more than half of his infantry brigades were yet to be closely engaged, while he had so far used but a portion of General Pendleton's artillery. He walked the night, hope rising again.

Yes: having failed on the right, then failed on the left, he would attack tomorrow dead center—there where the clump of trees rose from the crest of Cemetery Ridge against the indigo night sky—with George Pickett's division, fresh to the battlefield, leading the way.

The hot darkness groaned with the cries of the wounded, but he clenched his teeth and set forward anyway, canteens slung from either shoulder, to find the spring and the water. Everybody knew a spring was down there somewhere, at the foot of the hill they'd been trying to take, so he'd get there; he had to. He was thirsty him-

self, but the others were worse. Some would die without water. Some would die anyway.

He stumbled on in the direction they'd said, bumping into this figure or that in the deep violet evening, descending the curve of the ridge as he went. The smell of blood was in the air, and sweat, and somewhere a skunk. "Sorry," he said as he wove his way along, " 'scuse me, please," for he'd been raised to be polite. But he could hardly see where he was going, or whose camps he was moving through, and he knew he'd be lucky to get there at all, let alone get back if he did.

But he did, he got there, and somehow as he tumbled down the last slope to where the others lined up to take their turns filling at the spring he knew he'd return to his friends. The darkness by now was like ink, lightened only by the occasional flicker, through the trees, of a fire here or there. Someone jostled his arm and he turned.

"Oh," he said again, "sorry."

" 's all right."

"You been waiting long?"

"Long enough. Still . . . others here first."

He waited awhile; then he said, "You get hurt today?"

"Nope." The other waited. "You?"

"Me neither. Guess I was lucky. Lots did."

"Yep."

The other's turn came and he filled and left, saying, "See you," as he turned. Then it was his own turn and he took it, seven canteens in all, and started back for camp, wherever it was. Minutes passed, as he struggled up the curve of the ridge, before he caught on—

The voice should've told him, of course: the accent, the twang. He'd stood in line with a Yankee.

3

{ *Friday* }

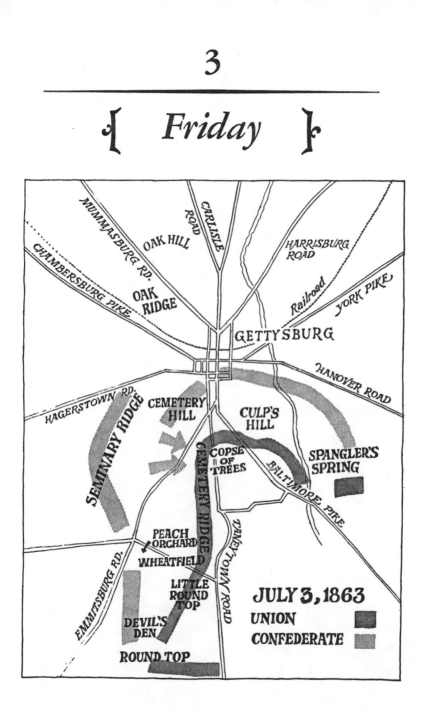

MUMMASBURG RD.

CARLISLE ROAD

CHAMBERSBURG PIKE

OAK HILL

HARRISBURG ROAD

OAK RIDGE

Railroad

YORK PIKE

GETTYSBURG

HANOVER ROAD

HAGERSTOWN RD.

CEMETERY HILL

CULP'S HILL

SEMINARY RIDGE

CEMETERY RIDGE

COPSE OF TREES

BALTIMORE PIKE

SPANGLER'S SPRING

PEACH ORCHARD

WHEATFIELD

EMMITSBURG RD.

TANEYTOWN ROAD

LITTLE ROUND TOP

DEVIL'S DEN

ROUND TOP

JULY 3, 1863

UNION

CONFEDERATE

THE MORNING SUN had cleared the ridges by eight, its unclouded brilliance foretelling a third torrid day for those doomed to fight beneath it, but long before that the shallow valley separating them and the armies occupying them was rank with the stench of decay. Throughout the night, while the exhausted survivors of Thursday's carnage slept by their weapons, litter-bearers roamed the meadows, wheatfield and peach orchard to bring in such of the wounded as the surgeons might hope still to save; but they abandoned more than they retrieved and most of those now were dead. Ripped and mangled bodies, few any longer distinguishable as Union or Confederate, began by dawn to bloat, and the carcasses of hundreds of horses, limbs severed, guts spilled, were swelling too; while the sweet, suffocating odor of them all was compounded by the dozens of hastily shoveled latrines, open to the air and used by thousands from both camps, crisscrossing the slopes of both ridges and the cluttered ground footing the Round Tops. Sunrise revealed it to be a valley of death: cruel, random and, for those trapped there, almost certainly inescapable.

Nonetheless Lee proposed to attack across it again, and to do so today. Already awake, dressed and breakfasted for hours, he determined as he rode south on Traveller to make the most of such advances as yesterday's assaults had brought and such strengths as he still possessed: Meade he'd wounded and yet might destroy, if he hit hard enough and persistently enough where he judged Meade weakest, in his center, and to that end he shaped and polished his plans as he sought out his warhorse, James Longstreet.

. . . Well, and if too, of course, he hit soon enough.

Already, it seemed, that doubt was valid. By now he should have come to anticipate that Longstreet would object, have a plan of his own, but with his usual grave courtesy Lee began by asking the other's view. Longstreet promptly gave it: his scouts, ranging the terrain throughout the night, reported excellent prospects still for maneuver south, to the right, around Meade's army, where they might then, on ground of their choice, await and receive attack. . . .

Deaf to him, Lee said, "No, general, no," his words echoing his argument of the day before, and pointed northeastward across the way. "The enemy is there, and I am going to strike him." His scheme was as simple as it was brutal. Between the two armies— each occupying its own long ridge parallel, north and south, to the other—lay a mile-wide vale of open pasturage bisected midway by the Emmitsburg Road. An initial bombardment by the concentrated power of 176 of Longstreet's guns would serve to drive Federal infantry and artillery out of their defensive lodgments on Cemetery Ridge; when it ended, the three brigades of Pickett's division and at least eight brigades detached from Heth's and Pender's divisions, the latter two usually part of Hill's corps, would advance from Seminary Ridge in a single broad wave across the valley, storm the enemy slope and converge like a flight of Agincourt arrows on the little clump of trees that marked its middle, there by shock and mass to break the Union line at last and detach its battered and demoralized fragments for separate destruction. Fifteen thousand men, Pickett's fresh and still unbloodied: and with their triumph the day—perhaps the war—would be theirs.

Longstreet's bulky form and brusque manner cloaked deep feeling and a broad empathy; he looked Lee in the eye and said deliberately, "General, I've been a soldier all my life. I've fought with soldiers in everything from couples, squads and companies to regiments, divisions and armies, and I know as well as anyone what soldiers can do." He breathed deeply. "And it's my opinion that no fifteen thousand men ever arrayed for battle could take that position."

Lee smiled—the sweet smile of a patient father for a stubborn son—and said, "Please send for General Pickett."

By then, at any rate, at least one of the principal subsidiary features of the day's program had already failed.

As partial protection for Pickett's advance on the Union center Lee's grand design had envisioned a strong diversionary assault on Meade's right by Ewell's soldiers, under Johnson, specifically against the defenses up Culp's Hill, a part of which they'd taken and kept the evening before, and he'd sent orders over to that effect. Dawn brought heavy firing from that direction, in fact, again raising his hope that success thereabouts must force Meade to divert troops from Cemetery Hill and in the process dilute his strength. But now the cannonade and musketry were ebbing and obviously soon would die, and shortly afterward word reached Lee that a fresh contingent of Federal reinforcements had come to the support of the hill's defenders and then ended matters by driving Johnson's soldiers away from Spangler's Spring and off the Culp's Hill area altogether. Thus Meade's right was safe, alas, and thus too —because it was safe—he could afford to concentrate his defenses at the point of Pickett's attack. Bad news, Lee thought, riding and reriding the length of his line: all of his remaining eggs lay in a single basket.

George Pickett would be carrying the basket, and when a few moments later he rode jauntily up, waving to friends as he passed and tipping his little blue cap to his commanders by way of salute, Lee's heavy spirits began again to lighten. Pickett was conspicuous, no question of that, and perhaps ambitious beyond any ability he'd so far demonstrated—last in his class at West Point and, though a dashing young hero vaulting the ramparts of Chapultepec in Mexico sixteen years ago, of little substantial battlefield experience since—but his peacock look and strut gave him a flair, a vivacity, that inspired enthusiasm and confidence in both his men and his superiors. Well, and now here he came, grinning through his curly mustache and short beard, his carefully cut uniform a tumult of gold buttons and braid, gold spurs twinkling against the sheen of his long black boots, perfumed brown hair falling in ringlets to his shoulder; and at the sight of him Lee broke into a warm welcoming smile, for this at last— as contrasted with the increasingly gloomy Longstreet— was a soldier thirsting for a fight.

He was about to get one too, as Lee promptly outlined, Longstreet meanwhile—whose immediate subordinate Pickett was, after all—listening silently, eyes downcast, alongside. Pickett should begin at once to align his three brigades within the woods extending the length of Seminary Ridge, then—when the preliminary cannonade died some time hence—move into the open and take the Union position up there on Cemetery Ridge where the little clump of trees lay; elements of Heth's division, under Pettigrew, and Pender's, under Trimble, would support his left, and Lang and Wilcox would cover his right from the peach orchard, but the brunt of the assault would be his. Was he ready? No soldier was ever more so, and giving a second salute to Lee and Longstreet, this time with his riding crop, Pickett spurred his horse and trotted eagerly off to settle details with his brigadiers.

That was heartening, at least to Lee, and with Pickett's departure he was free to turn to preparation of the artillery bombardment by which he intended to ease the subsequent infantry advance; and in fact he found Longstreet's youthful chief gunner, a Georgia colonel named Alexander, already busily moving his pieces northward from the peach orchard in an arc that, by the time he'd completed his dispositions, extended most of a mile till it reached Lee's own command post near the center of the ridge. There it met, end to end, a second matching arc of guns from Hill's corps, these sweeping still further north almost to the Chambersburg Pike, the eventual result being an immense crescent of artillery two miles long and stretching nearly the length of Seminary Ridge, 176 guns in all, and all aimed with deadly concentration at the clump of trees opposite where Lee proposed to strike his deathblow. Alexander, moreover, would signal the opening of fire throughout the crescent; and—though as an officer of relatively junior rank he was troubled by Longstreet's order to do so—he'd also instruct Pickett when the cannonade had driven off the Yanks and the infantry might move forward. Already, he sensed, Longstreet was moving to disassociate himself from an action he believed doomed, though for the moment the sheer work of seeing his batteries sited and sighted, and sufficient ammunition to fuel them stacked alongside, left him time to take no more than token exception.

Still, it all took time, time as precious today as yesterday, when so much had been wasted; and as he rode back and forth along the edge of the woods Lee fretted to himself at how quickly the day was passing without real action. Every moment of preparation for attack, he knew, must make possible an identical moment of preparation for defense, so that what he gained by painstaking care here must be offset by what he lost in allowing equally painstaking care over there. His intuition, his instinct—call it what one would: perhaps it was really his experience—told him the crucial weakness in Meade's line lay where the clump of trees marked the center of the ridge; but he could not confirm it, could not *know*, except through the test of battle. Yet the matter was thicker than that, after all: Meade was as cautious as he himself was audacious, but not without a cunning of his own, and it was not inconceivable that, reading Lee's intention, he'd bolster his defenses precisely where Lee'd attack. . . .

Well, but those were the imponderables that made war so fascinating, so *beautiful*—terrible though it was too, of course. Meanwhile here were his soldiers, the gunners stripped to their waists as they readied their cannon, chests oily with sweat in the rising heat of midday, then behind them, out of sight in the woods and the ravine beyond, the magnificent infantry—Jim Kemper's Virginians, Dick Garnett's, Lewis Armistead's—Pickett's troops all, and all of them ready; while further north still Pettigrew's four brigades and Trimble's two were filing into place, men from North Carolina, Tennessee, Alabama, Mississippi, a cross section, as it were, of the Confederacy itself.

Yet it was a cross section, too, of a wounded land, for as he rode slowly north through the woods, then south again, Lee could not help but see the damage wrought already by this accidental battle into which he had led his army. Far too many soldiers preparing even now to attack wore bandages about their heads and arms and legs, some so swaddled in bloody rags they showed only one eye, some unable to walk without support; far too many were shoeless, and all were stringily, hungrily lean of limb and gaunt of face. A fever was passing among them as well, and though it and the broiling summer sun combined to make them almost unbearably hot, Dick Garnett was aligning his brigade muffled knee to neck in a heavy blue overcoat against the chills that intermittently brought shudders to his body, and the seeming eccentricity of his garb was echoed here and there by others. Nor were all the wounds Lee witnessed visible: gradually, weaving his way from one regiment to the next, he began to grasp how thin the ranks of many had become, how far heavier the first two days' losses were than he'd realized —indeed, he silently calculated, he'd be lucky to send in ten thousand today, a serious reduction from the fifteen thousand he'd intended. His chest tightened, elbow throbbed. They must strike soon, then, and strike well, for his reserves—and the South's—were scant against failure.

. . . But *no:* he could not contemplate failure, he would not—the Army of Northern Virginia, he told himself again, could do anything, anything—and with an impatient nudge he touched Traveller's flank and cantered off to the edge of the woods. His soldiers quietened and lifted their hats as he passed, and as was his way he returned the salute in kind. Men so devoted could *never* fail.

III

He reached his command post again in time to see a house and barn burn midway between the two ridges, set afire by Yank skirmishers sent to clear them of the Confederate sharpshooters who'd occupied and used them to murderous effect since dawn; then, with his staff, he waited in the long quiet time that followed for the bombardment to begin. Few spoke, and then in hushed voices. Lee's dispositions were complete: the guns were arrayed and required only Longstreet's signal to open, while behind them, still hidden by the woods, the nine brigades of infantry whose butternut ranks George Pickett presently would lead across the valley sweated in the noontime heat as they bided their time; now the issue rested with God.

The guns spoke first. Shortly past one, two pieces near the center of the great artillery arc struck the tocsin, whereupon—after a sharp instant of silence as premonitory as the cry of a wolf—the entire two miles of line erupted in a roar unlike anything anyone on either side had ever heard. One by one, then, the individual four-gun batteries fired by salvo, pitching their varied missiles onto Cemetery Ridge in immense trajectories of metal that whistled as they fell. Solid shot, hollow shells that exploded over or on their targets, shrapnel that when detonated scattered loads of musket balls upon the enemy, canister—all were in use and all deadly; and though the smoke quickly gathered about the bucking guns, Lee could see through the openings between them that the bluecoats were scurrying to find cover on the hillside opposite. Load, ram, fire, sponge, load, ram, fire, sponge, on and on, din and action continuous, flame spewing eastward from one end of Seminary Ridge to the other . . . it was as he'd conceived it. Good hunting, he thought: let this sublime mass succeed.

The question remained open, however. Once they'd absorbed the initial shock of Lee's barrage, Meade's infantry began to creep back into their rifle pits along the near side of Cemetery Ridge, stunned but resilient, and soon thereafter his gunners began to answer the bombardment with one of their own. First from the high ground of Little Round Top, then from the opposite end of the Union position at Cemetery Hill, a steady counterfire of solid shot and exploding shell began to rain upon the woods of Seminary Ridge, particularly devastating, as soon became evident, because it caught Lee's waiting riflemen in a crossfire from which they could find no easy escape; the Yanks were overshooting, it seemed, their missiles falling well beyond their apparent target of the Confederate guns, but by ironic accident they were doing greater damage to troops of whose disposition and plans they presumably were unaware than to those at whose lodgments their batteries were aimed.

Were his own guns overshooting too? Lee could hardly help wondering, but in the chaotic confusion of barrage and counterbarrage he had no way of knowing, for the dense clouds of smoke covering most of the battleground made careful observation by either side equally impossible. Casualties aplenty were only too visible, though, among Alexander's gunners unlucky enough to catch the odd Yank shells falling their way, more dramatically along the ranks and rows of Pickett's infantry, and Pettigrew's and Trimble's, all huddled in the woods and behind them awaiting the signal to rise and advance . . . which, considering the losses they were taking here in motionless readiness, could come no better than sooner. Yes, but Longstreet had worked that out: Alexander would pass the word when he believed assault propitious.

. . . And then at last the word came. Nearing two forty-five, the Union guns fell suddenly silent, and from his observation post on a slight hummock of earth near the peach orchard, Alexander could see through his glasses that at least a few were being withdrawn from the

83

center of Cemetery Ridge—the very sign he'd been waiting for, he told himself, sure evidence his bombardment had succeeded in thinning Meade's defenses there, and promptly dashed off a note to George Pickett. "For God's sake come quick," it said, "or my ammunition will not let me support you properly."

By the time it reached Pickett the Confederate batteries had ceased firing too, to cool, to save shells, to ready themselves to cover his charge, so he rode off to find Longstreet in the hush that now enveloped the battlefield, a jaunty cavalier on a spirited horse, watched at that moment by everyone. That was gratifying, but Longstreet's gloominess was not. He sat astride the snake-rail fence at the edge of the woods absently whittling as he gazed across the valley to where the Yanks waited, a big man whose sorrows and doubts matched his frame, and his despairing look said everything.

"Shall I advance, general?" Pickett asked as Longstreet finished reading Alexander's note.

Longstreet slowly raised his head, and Pickett was astonished to see his old friend's cheeks glistening with tears. Longstreet stammered a moment, then said haltingly, "I don't want to make this charge. I don't see how it can succeed." He paused again. "But General Lee ordered it and expects it. . . ."

Pickett's voice cracked as he said, "Yes, Pete, but am I to go forward?"

Longstreet's eyes fell. Silently, heavily, he nodded.

"Then I move up at once, sir," Pickett said, and

snapped off a brisk salute before remounting. As he turned the corner of the woods he saw Longstreet still sitting there, motionless, downcast, as he'd found and left him.

That was puzzling enough—not like Old Peter to shun a fight, he thought, not his way at all—but the sight of his own soldiers awaiting his return quickly stilled the tremor of apprehension their conversation had started; and indeed, within another minute or two, he and they were all action again. To his signal they now arose and began forming and dressing their ranks, tough and leathery in their butternut homespun, high smelling and formidable, checking their muskets one final time, slipping bayonets into place, chewing, spitting, hawking, elbowing one another in the joshing way of men about to go under fire; while up the line to the north the troops of Pettigrew's and Trimble's commands, their companions in the coming assault, made similar preparations.

The hour of three struck and passed. The afternoon sun bore down mercilessly. Then the smoke enveloping the field drifted off and they stepped into the open. Pickett rode forward to the center of his division and waved his saber in the direction of Cemetery Ridge. "To the charge!" he cried, and wheeled his horse. "Don't forget today that you're from old Virginia!" Pettigrew, meanwhile, was pointing his soldiers the same way. "Now, Colonel," he told the commander of his advance brigade of Carolinians, "for the honor of the good Old North State, forward!"

And so it was: forward they went, ten thousand and more, in a great gray wave a mile across from south to north, the bright, varied colors of the ensigns of forty-two separate regiments from Virginia, North Carolina, Tennessee, Alabama and Mississippi snapping at intervals against the slight breeze raised by their steady pace eastward. The gleam of their bayonets made a glittering forest above the brown meadow; their cups and canteens jingled to their steps; and as they advanced the rustle of their feet against the stubble of pasturage kicked up dust and chaff like spray before the prow of a ship. Left, right, left, right, they strode, the sergeants counting cadence, file closers shouting orders to join ranks where small gaps developed here and there, while at the forefront of his brigade Lewis Armistead plucked off his broad-brimmed black felt hat, fixed it to the point of his saber and raised it skyward to signal his direction; ahead of him Dick Garnett led them all, still tightly wrapped within his overcoat, because of his fever the only officer on the field allowed to ride . . . and thus of them all the most dramatically exposed.

Irresistible, thought Lee, watching them alone from a seat he'd made for himself by spreading a sheet of oilcloth across an old stump at the edge of the woods; no army on earth—no army ever—could halt that valorous array. . . .

By now the Army of the Potomac thought otherwise, however. Pickett's division had scarcely passed its own arc of guns when the Union batteries on the Round Tops, survivors of yesterday's fighting, began to rain shell into Kemper's brigade, its rightmost flank, and hardly a moment later Mayo's brigade a mile to the north on the furthermost left began taking equally brutal punishment from a cluster of Federal cannon on Cemetery Hill—enfilading fire in both cases and equally murderous, it soon became evident, because shells missing their primary targets plowed on to inflict the same damage or worse on the next regiments in line. Then, near the well of the valley, Mayo's men came under closeup rifle fire from an undetected concentration of Yank infantry on their left, and in the ensuing panic their ranks broke and scattered and within moments all four regiments were fleeing pell-mell for the rear.

From his own vantage point atop the snake-rail fence Longstreet watched the rapidly mounting destruction of his forces with horror and despair—it was even worse than he'd foreseen, and what he'd foreseen was terrible enough—and when a visiting English officer observing the charge rode up and exclaimed, "I wouldn't've missed this for anything!" Longstreet gave a bitter laugh as he answered, "The devil you wouldn't! I'd like to've missed it very much. Look there: we've attacked and been repulsed."

By now, though, he was as powerless to halt the tragedy as he'd been to dissuade Lee from creating it. Pickett's division had begun to bear left to close its distance from Pettigrew's and to better its aim on the clump of trees that was its target, but the more oblique its direction became the more completely it exposed its right flank to the Union guns on the Round Tops and to the Yank rifles on the south end of Cemetery Ridge. Kemper's ranks were thinning quickly, as a result, and Garnett's to Kemper's left; and though the gaps were closed promptly, every fresh yard of advance was being won with fewer men. Even from half a mile back and through the rapidly gathering smoke Longstreet could see what a devastating cost in killed and wounded the entire assault was exacting.

Yet on it went. Along the crest of Cemetery Ridge its defenders had drawn their bluecoated infantry and artillery into a tightly concentrated crescent before and around the clump of trees, skirmishers in place well out front beyond and along the low stone wall that broke the slope, and were firing point-blank and with deadly effect into the Confederate ranks sweeping slowly toward them from the valley below. Then Pickett's men halted alongside Pettigrew's to realign—what had begun as an attack wave a mile wide from end to end had now contracted, by convergence, to a shapeless mass no more than five hundred yards across—and as they idled there at the roadway bisecting the valley, tearing down the fences siding the road and trying to dress their lines and restore some degree of formation before starting their final rush up the hill, they presented an even denser target to the Union guns, which promptly began to pour round after round of canister directly into their midst.

Losses again were cruel, but the pause at least was brief, for though companies and even regiments of both divisions were by then hopelessly intertangled, making further systematic command of individual units impossible, their leaders saw no choice was left them, if they were to escape slaughter where they stood, but to move at once; and when their brigadiers began to mill amongst them shouting orders to fire, then charge, it proved to be the signal for which all had waited. With a crash their muskets spoke at last, volley upon volley, and then, screeching their eerie yell, they bolted headlong up the slope.

Order had vanished; only motion and momentum remained as the armies locked in a pandemonium of flaming muzzles and struggling bodies. Fry fell, wounded in the thigh, then Garnett, shot dead from his horse, still wrapped in his overcoat as he plummeted to the ground; and a moment afterward Kemper went down too, a bullet in his groin, and Marshall, killed rallying his brigade. Yet some few stood on to surge up the slope toward the trees, perhaps three hundred or more, and among them, pushing his way to the forefront to assume their leadership now that Garnett and Kemper were gone, was Armistead, white hair and beard flying, black hat held high on the blade of his saber. . . . "Come on!" he cried, and they poured forward behind him into the Federal fire, now coming at them from three sides, musketry, canister, pistol fire; then they were nearing and suddenly reached the stone wall, the Yank riflemen were falling back as they came up, and Armistead stepped across, signaling the survivors to follow. They did too, ranks thinning with every step, into fighting so close friend and foe were no longer distinguishable, a brutal thing of bayonets and musket butts and even stones and clubs rudely clutched from the litter underfoot, while to the north, to their left, the remnants of Pettigrew's division, fleshed out by a handful of stragglers from Trimble's, strove in similar disarray to cross a further section of the wall.

Union cannon fire was now at a range so short its effect was that of a gigantic shotgun, and fresh Yank reinforcements were funneling into the struggle behind and around the batteries; but the sheer force of Armistead's uphill charge had borne him and his men so deeply inside the angle of the wall that for a moment, when a complement of Federal gunners dropped their sponges and cut for the rear, their triumph seemed inevitable. That proved no truer than any other of the day's many delusions, however. Armistead himself—stepping forward, hand extended, to claim one of the enemy guns—abruptly staggered and fell, body and leg riddled with bullets; and with his fall the desperate last dash his example had fired as abruptly broke and ended. Here and there within the angle some few of his followers fought stubbornly on until killed or overcome; and more, all but surrounded, prudently threw up their hands in surrender; but most, facing the certainty of defeat, dropped their muskets and turned and bolted back down the slope; and the Yanks, as exhausted as they, let them go with only a token parting shot or two. It was over: the wave of Pickett's charge had reached its high-water mark short of the clump of trees, then receded, and for those who'd survived it only a safe withdrawal to the relative security of Seminary Ridge and the wooded vale to its rear any longer mattered.

For James Longstreet, however, watching in unsurprised despair as the bloody remnants of his favorite division, and their comrades from Pettigrew's and Trimble's, streamed slowly, sullenly back across the Emmitsburg Road, then up the long meadow to where he waited, the defeat was not only tragic—and unnecessary—but the source of possible additional disaster to them all. After so signal a victory, Meade would be a fool not to counterattack at once—he would himself, at any rate, were their roles reversed—so he must brace his reserves, or what was left of them, to take the blow . . . and so must Hill, and Ewell; and Lee, though surely by now he'd've foreseen the same likelihood, must be warned that his army now lay in imminent danger of nothing less than destruction. Ironic, that: yesterday, he remembered grimly—*today, for God's sake!*—Lee'd talked blandly of destroying Meade.

Still, recrimination was a luxury for which he now had neither time nor inclination—the imperative priority was to bring in such survivors as remained and thereby to salvage as much of the army as possible. He dispatched couriers to instruct Wilcox and Lang to cover the retreat with their brigades, then rode forward himself to speed the thousands of men fleeing toward him on foot; and as they neared he began to feel the full force of the catastrophe he'd both predicted and watched, though until then only from afar. Whatever discipline they'd once boasted was gone: they raced up the long slope like frightened hares, eyes sightless for anything but the trees at the crest of the ridge, casting off canteens and muskets and shell boxes as they came. Almost all bore some sign of injury, heads, arms or legs bloodily wrapped against their wounds, shirts or jeans cut or torn, and many, staggering on with the aid of crutches improvised from sticks or up-turned muskets, seemed unlikely to make the course. George Pickett himself trotted past on his big black horse, face shining with tears, blind to Longstreet. Around them in every direction the bodies of the dead seemed literally to cover the ground. Longstreet shook his huge head angrily and moved on. In twenty years as a soldier he'd seen nothing worse.

Recriminations? No. But he knew whom to blame.

V

Meanwhile Lee had remounted too and was riding Traveller at a slow walk toward the rout. His face, so often red with excitement, was ashen; his voice was a whisper; the pain in his chest had been replaced by a kind of deathly numbness . . . appropriately enough, for he'd just suffered a kind of death: his pride, his confidence, whatever it was that gave him the arrogance it took to command a great army—the conviction of invincibility, perhaps, perhaps the conviction of his own infallibility.

Believing them capable of anything, he'd asked more of his soldiers than they could give; they'd failed him.

Or else—a darker possibility—he'd asked more of them than could be given, than existed, in which case he'd failed them.

Either way—

"It is all my fault," he began saying to himself, then aloud to the soldiers streaming past, poor shattered, wounded, frightened children as they'd become, ". . . my fault, my fault," and at the recognition of his stricken sympathy for their plight many slowed and—what they did for no one else—lifted their hats. He nodded gravely and bade them on.

Pettigrew came by, badly injured, and Kemper, borne on a litter, and for both he had words of solace and encouragement—they must hasten to mend, he assured them, for he would need their counsel and leadership in the difficult days ahead—then finally, desolate, George Pickett, eyes red with weeping.

Lee waited, said softly, "General, place your division in rear of this hill and be ready to repel the advance of the enemy should they follow up their advantage."

Pickett stammered; drew breath again; managed

at last to say, "Sir, I have no division now. Armistead's down . . . Garnett's down . . . Kemper's mortally wounded," and halted there, mouthing soundlessly a horror he could express no further.

"Come, come, General Pickett," Lee said calmly. "This has been my fight, and upon my shoulders rests the blame." He paused, sighed. "Your men have done all men can do. The fault is entirely my own."

. . . Calmly, soothingly, reassuringly: so he spoke now as he made his way through the ragged remains of his defeated army—"All this has been my fault," he told Wilcox, "It is I who have lost this fight, and you must help me out of it the best way you can," while to a handful of scarecrow infantrymen limping painfully to the rear he said, "All this will come right in the end. Meantime we want all good and true men just now"—for Meade's counterattack, he was confident, must come soon.

Yet it did not. By late afternoon he'd succeeded in forming a firm defense line of five brigades across the center of Seminary Ridge, and with his cavalry finally reassembled and his artillery intact he believed he could withstand all but the most determined assault from across the way. Stocks of ammunition were dwindling, to be sure, and food was low, but he was prepared to effect his retreat in good order even should Meade—as seemed to him, as to Longstreet, inevitable—seek to block him.

That he had no real choice now but to retreat was unarguable—his army was wounded too deeply, had fought itself out—and as night fell he turned to making his plans, then rode off to give Longstreet, Hill and Ewell their orders: they must hold their present positions tomorrow, allowing the wounded a day's start on the long road back to Virginia, and begin their own marches, Hill leading, after dark. . . . Was all clear? It was, and with a fleeting smile of regret for the catastrophe to which he'd brought them he bowed and returned to his tent alongside the Chambersburg Pike. He was very weary, felt very old—thought abruptly of his father's ruin, tried to remember his face, failed. It had been a sad day, a terrible day, and no one's hands were bloodier for it than his.

Yet his puzzlement remained—why he? why here? —and before he lay down at last to seek a moment's sleep from the fitful restlessness wracking his body and brain he stepped outside to walk slowly in the moonlight one final time in Gettysburg; and there, clapping his hands softly, he said as if to the night, "Too bad, too bad. Oh, too bad!"

The ridge was up there somewhere, he knew it was, it had to be, and he told himself again and again that if he could only get back to it he'd live. It was where they'd started, where the army was, where the doctors were, and he must make himself get there.

It was hard, though, the hardest thing he'd ever tried. All that remained of his left arm was a white shank of bone with a few rags of flesh and flannel hanging loose from it, and something was wrong with his stomach besides—his middle was so bloody he couldn't tell what, but that last blast point-blank from the Yank cannon had caught him with the rest. The rest it had killed, of course; he'd taken fire on the edge of the pattern, so still stood.

Well, crawled. He'd staggered off when it happened, he and whatever others were left, back out of the angle in the rock fence, and though his head was swimming he'd made it down the slope and crossed the road upright. Then he'd fallen, he must've, for now he was trying to pull himself along, with his one good arm, back up the ridge he'd descended so proudly that afternoon. But it was dark now, or seemed dark, and smoke was everywhere, and he couldn't be sure of his bearings. . . .

It was darker still when he came to again. On either side he could hear cries and moans, but he could see nothing, nothing, and he pulled himself on, crawling like a baby, in what he could only guess must be the way. What would his father think to see him now?

At least he'd stopped hurting, almost stopped feeling, but it was so hard, so hard, and maybe, just a minute there, he'd rest; yes. And again; yes. And again—

And then it didn't matter. Nothing mattered. Nothing hurt or bothered him. He rolled over onto his back and stared into the night as it descended to envelop him.

"Mother," he whispered.

Epilogue

I T WAS WORSE THAN THAT: worse than Longstreet had predicted: worse than either had believed possible.

Morning, the beginning of what threatened to be another insufferable day of heat, humidity and the stench of death on every side, brought the first dependable accounting of Friday's disasters, and as the figures came in from the company and regimental roll calls up and down the line Lee felt the last of his confidence leave him. He did not see how he—or they—could go on.

The toll was intolerable. Half of the eleven thousand infantrymen he'd sent forward on that doomed last charge under Pickett and Pettigrew had fallen, were killed or captured, and when the number of wounded from both bombardment and assault were added, the day's casualties rose to more than seventy-five hundred—60 percent of the twelve thousand five hundred troops engaged sunrise to sunset. The tragedy was one of quality as well as quantity, moreover. All three of Pickett's brigadiers were gone, Garnett and Armistead forever, twelve of his fifteen regimental commanders were dead and the rest wounded, and above 60 percent of his foot soldiers had been lost between the two ridges; and Pettigrew's subtractions were nearly as bad in both number and kind. The lesson was cruel and humbling, and as with a grave face Lee took the reports one by one from his staff and did the awful arithmetic he saw at last that the butcher's bill was not only too high but had taken the cream of his army; he was wasting its leadership.

Nor was that all. The true measure of his losses must include not only Friday's casualties but those since he'd first given battle two days earlier, west of Gettysburg, and at those figures his heart turned over. A third of the fifty-two general officers he'd brought north were gone, five of them dead, three captured and nine wounded, and no fewer than eighteen of his colonels had been killed or taken prisoner, so that the toll his campaign had taken of its commanders stretched past the immediate crisis into the future. Not even that grim truth could surpass for horror the totals for the army as a whole, however. Though they must yet be considered incomplete and un-official, Lee's own estimates this miserable morning appalled him: since crossing the Potomac he'd lost twenty thousand of the seventy-five thousand men whose ranks comprised the Army of Northern Virginia, most of them from the sixty thousand riflemen of the three infantry corps, and when the numbers of captured were compiled dependably, he suspected, the cost in manpower—no, in *lives*—must climb far higher.

He shook his head mutely. No doubt Meade had suffered too, perhaps as cruelly, but Union resources were endless; the South's were near exhaustion.

Like his men.

Like him.

There his mind paused, unable for a moment to take whatever next step it should, till a staff officer—young Taylor, it must have been—gently reminded him of the anticipated counterattack. He nodded absently. He was ready, or his reserves were, or as ready as was possible. Neither he nor they could do more, and meanwhile the long train of wounded had moved off south. God's will be done. . . .

As no doubt it had.

But then eleven came, and noon, and he could see or hear no sign of Federal activity, nor could his outposts; and when a heavy rainfall began about one and went on and on into the early twilight, drenching them all and turning the brooks and branches on every side into quick streams running dark with the blood washing into them from the slopes of the ridges, Lee concluded his withdrawal was safe. True to his history, Meade had chosen caution above risk, though risk might in fact have won him the war then and there; and though Lee recognized with relief the removal of the first obstacle to his retreat, something in him sighed to do so. Going on—now inevitable—offered no prospect but . . . more.

Hill and Ewell came by to take their leaves, which were brief, then vanished into the storm to dispose their forces, and Stuart looked in a moment too before departing, still contrite for his dereliction but all the more firmly determined to make his screen of their long train homeward impenetrable; and finally Longstreet, Old Peter, huge, dark, heavy with defeat but as dogged as ever in his dutiful loyalty. Lee saw the mixture of love and sorrow in his eyes, took his hand briefly and sent him on, grateful there'd been no word of reproach. No man deserved it more.

So at last he was ready himself. Traveller came—another case of stubborn loyalty, and he thanked God for it —and he mounted and started slowly up the muddy line of walking wounded and ambulance wagons slogging slowly south. What had gone wrong? Everything, everything: Jackson's death, Stuart's absence and silence, Hill's reluctance, Ewell's hesitation, Longstreet's slows; but most of all—central and crucial, ineradicable and unforgivable —himself, his judgment, his rigidity, his pride. They had exacted a price he scarcely dared face, though he must.

He tapped Traveller's flank and trotted forward. Ahead the line of retreat snaked into the dim, rainy distance. He could not see the end.

No one who presumes nowadays to
write about the three days of
Gettysburg is without debt to
those who've gone before; and
it is a particular pleasure for
me to acknowledge the obligation
I have to the fundamental work
of Douglas Freeman, Bruce Catton,
Clifford Dowdey and Shelby Foote.
Three additional volumes of enormous
interest and value are
Joseph E. Persico's *My Enemy, My
Brother: Men and Days of Gettysburg,*
William A. Frassanito's
Gettysburg: A Journey in Time
and Michael Shaara's incomparable
novel, *The Killer Angels.*